D O V

Folk
Tales

DOWN

FOLK TALES

STEVE LALLY

The History Press Ireland

This book is dedicated to my beautiful little daughter, Isabella Grace, for she is the measure of my dreams.

I would also like to dedicate this book to the memory of my father, Patrick John Lally, 1945-1993, who always believed in me.

And my grandmother, Margaret Power-King, who died in 1982, who was both a great storyteller and inspiration.

Finally to my friend Peter Shortall, who sadly passed through 'the etheral wall' in 2011. 'I did it Shortie!'

First published 2013, reprinted 2016

The History Press Ireland
50 City Quay
Dublin 2
Ireland
www.thehistorypress.ie

© Steve Lally, 2013
Illustrations © Steve Lally, 2013

The right of Steve Lally to be identified as the Author
of this work has been asserted in accordance with the
Copyright, Designs and Patents Act 1988.

British Library Cataloguing in Publication Data.
A catalogue record for this book is available from the British Library.

ISBN 978 1 84588 758 2

Typesetting and origination by The History Press

CONTENTS

Acknowledgements

Jason Diamond, Genealogy and Heritage Officer, Banbridge District Council, for pointing me in the right direction.

All the staff at the Banbridge Library, County Down.

Evelyn Hanna, area manager, Libraries NI.

Briege Stitt at the Heritage Gallery in Downpatrick Library, County Down.

The staff at the Millennium Court Art Centre for all their support.

Emma Hirsk for the use of her laptop.

Liz Weir, master storyteller and mentor, for her inspiration and salvation.

Seamus McCormick and the Sacred Heart Boxing Club
'Descended from Kings!'

Ciaran Gallagher, artist, for photographing and
documenting all the illustrations.

Kevin Woods, 'The Leprechaun Whisperer'.

My good friend Florian Schanz for all his wisdom.

Jon and Tracy Barker, for their Keen and Golden Eye.

James Fulton, for his enthusiasm and friendship.

Evi O'Halloran for her enlightenment and guidance.

Miss Paula Flynn, my Little Star burning bright.

All the staff and childrn at the Royal Victoria Hospital for
Sick Children, Belfast. You are an inspiration.

To all my family and friends.

Lastly, but by no means least, I would like to
thank all those who ever listened to me tell a story,
booked me and believed in me, as without you this
would all still be a dream.

1

THE RAPPAREE: REDMOND O'HANLON

A shepherd that lives in Slieve Gullion
Came down to the County Tyrone.
And told us how Redmond O'Hanlon
Won't leave the rich Saxon alone.
He rides over moorland and mountain,
By night, till a stranger is found,
Saying, 'Take your own choice to be lodging
Right over or under the ground!'

(From 'Redmond O'Hanlon' by Patrick Joseph McCall)

It's said that the first of the legendary English 'highwaymen' were royalist officers who 'took to the road' when they were outlawed under the Commonwealth. These were men familiar with the relatively newfangled pistols, which gave them an advantage over their victims, armed only with swords.

Perhaps because they concentrated on the wealthy, the highwaymen became popular heroes. No one, except the victims, grieved when the dukes and lords were held up with the immortal words, 'Stand and deliver, your money or your life'. In fact, some of these infamous highwaymen such as Dick Turpin, James Maclaine and Claude Duval held a celebrity status.

Here in Ireland we had our own legendary highwaymen known as 'rapparees' and 'tories' (*Toraidhe*). Both names are of Irish origin, the former meaning 'plunderers or destroyers' and the latter signifying that such outlaws who committed these heinous crimes were 'hunted' or 'wanted men'.

These men were products of the confiscation of lands from the native Irish. These dispossessed landowners were, to say the least, vengeful and many of them, like their English counterparts, were trained in the art of war.

They took themselves to the nearest woods, bogs or mountains, and honed their martial skills in order to bring down the unwelcome foreigners.

There was no mercy shown to these outlaws; they were pursued, hunted down and shot when captured. Their heads carried off to obtain rewards that were offered by the English rulers. Official documents state that this was a thing of weekly, sometimes daily, occurrence.

Of all the Rapparees of Ireland, the most famous, was Redmond O'Hanlon (*c.* 1620-25 April 1681). His name and his deeds are still vividly remembered today in the counties of Louth, Armagh, Monaghan and of course County Down. The writer William Carleton made him the central character of his 1862 novel *Redmond Count O'Hanlon: The Irish Rapparee*. But Carleton's story is mainly fiction, smattered with facts and loosely based on O'Hanlon's life.

O'Hanlon was one of those 'noble fugitives' driven into rebellion and transgression by English policy in Ireland. He was the chief of Orior, in County Armagh, claimed to be hereditary royal standard-bearer north of the Boyne. He was the son of Loughlin O'Hanlon, rightful heir to Tandragee Castle, now home to the popular snack food 'Tayto Crisps'.

In 1653, under the Parliament of the Commonwealth, the O'Hanlon lands were taken from them and the family was sent to Connacht, where they received a small pittance of land. At the Restoration in 1660, Hugh O'Hanlon petitioned to have their lands restored, but this was in vain.

Redmond O'Hanlon, probable brother of Hugh, took to the hills, vowing 'vengeance, black and bitter' against the 'Horde of Undertakers' that now held the best lands in Ulster. Many other dispossessed Irishmen flocked to his banner. Amongst these men were Protestant landlords, militia officers, and even Anglican and Catholic priests, who would work as informal members of his gang, giving him inside information and casing places for him to raid.

For twenty years he kept the settlers in the counties of Louth, Armagh, Monaghan and Down in terror. Many of the big farmers were paying him regular contributions for protection from all other tories. A letter from the era states that O'Hanlon's activities were bringing in more money than the King's revenue collectors. He was as shrewd a businessman as he was a bandit.

According to letters by St Oliver Plunkett, O'Hanlon increased in public favour as the colonial militia who were sent to capture him spent more time looting and pillaging the peasantry than actively looking for him. Those who did come across him did not live to tell the tale. It seemed that none would oppose him either through loyalty, admiration or fear.

It is said that O'Hanlon was never outwitted, except for one time by a country lad who was servant to a merchant

shopkeeper in Dundalk, County Louth. This merchant
had a debt of a couple of hundred pounds owed to him by
another merchant in Newry, County Down. The Dundalk
man wanted the money, but Redmond O'Hanlon held the
country between Dundalk and Newry and so no man with
either money or valuables would dare pass through that way.

The servant lad who worked for the Dundalk merchant
had often heard his master complain and moan about the
fact he could not get his money, so he offered to go to
Newry to collect the debt. The master had perfect faith in
the youth's honesty and integrity, but would not hear of
such a dangerous and insane proposal.

But many months passed by and the young man's self-
confidence and eagerness for adventure kept growing and
in the end his master consented to his undertaking the
dangerous mission.

He supplied the boy with pistols and ammunition, but to
his surprise the boy insisted on taking an old slow-going grey
nag, instead of the best racehorse in the stables. The youth set
out and in less than half an hour he found himself winding
his way through the craggy trails of the Fews Mountains. He
was in no hurry and he whistled as he went, for he wanted
to be seen. He travelled a long distance without meeting
a single soul, kept company only by the wind rustling the
leaves on the trees, the sound of his horse's hooves trudging
below him and the occasional cry from a wild animal or bird.

He was beginning to fear that his plan might fail, when
he heard the sound of thundering hooves, and soon saw the
notorious Redmond O'Hanlon dashing towards him. He was
mounted on a magnificent black stallion. The boy feigned
fear and even made a weak attempt to gallop back home on
the old mare, but in a moment O'Hanlon was beside him.

He asked the lad who he was, where he was coming from and what the purpose of his journey was. The boy answered all these questions frankly and truly and with every expression of great innocence. Then he confidently told his interrogator that there was just one thing he was afraid of, and that was being robbed by Redmond O'Hanlon.

The stranger assured him that he would protect him from this danger and having asked the boy when he expected to return, the boy told him with every show of confidence.

The youth was then given free passage and made his way to Newry, where he got the money for his master. Before returning, however, he got two or three pounds changed into copper, which he carried in a large leather bag, holding the remainder of the money secretly on his person. Then he proceeded to make his way home and, as expected, he encountered O'Hanlon again at the appointed meeting place.

On learning that he had got the money, O'Hanlon demanded the cash at once. The poor boy pleaded hard, but in vain. O'Hanlon produced his pistol and uttered the words, 'Stand and deliver, your money or your life'. At last, with an air of desperation, the boy shouted, 'Well, it shall never be said I handed you my master's money', and so saying, he flung the leather bag across a high hedge (some say a high wall).

The coins jingled as the bag fell and O'Hanlon dismounted his horse with ease, impressed by the lad's courage and yet totally deceived by his apparent naivety. No sooner had he crossed the hedge or wall, the boy slipped from his old mare and jumped on O'Hanlon's powerful stallion and was off like the wind. Behind him he left a bewildered O'Hanlon with a useless horse and a bag full of coppers.

In William Carleton's novel, *Redmond Count O'Hanlon: The Irish Rapparee*, he mentions this story and claims that O'Hanlon's horse was put into a livery in Dundalk and advertised. O'Hanlon never claimed him, but instead wrote a letter (unsigned) to the lad's master, stating that the horse's owner made a present of him to the 'young rogue' in reward for his cleverness and ingenuity. Carlton also states that O'Hanlon could never tell the story without laughing heartily and 'wishin' he had the trainin' of the lad'.

O'Hanlon's escapades and adventures continued for a brave few years after this incident. But things were to take a turn for the worse for the outlaw. O'Hanlon had an undying hatred for Anglo-Irish landowner Henry St John, who had been granted the traditional lands of the O'Hanlon clan. This hatred deepened when St John began evicting O'Hanlon's clansmen in large numbers. A private war between the men and their forces raged. The first major casualty of this war was St John's nineteen-year-old son, who was killed by the O'Hanlon gang on 9 September 1679. Outraged by this, James Butler, 1st Duke of Ormonde, the 'Lord Deputy of Ireland', ordered the assassination of Redmond O'Hanlon.

The duke's warrant was issued to Mr William Lucas, a planter and militia officer from Dromantine, who in turn recruited Arthur 'Art' MacCall O'Hanlon to carry out the assassination. Art was Redmond O'Hanlon's foster brother and close associate but was of a treacherous and avaricious nature.

According to the Revd H.W. Lett, who wrote about O'Hanlon in the 1898 edition of the *Banbridge Household Almanac*, when the order for his death was brought about, Redmond assigned two bodyguards to be at his side at all times, these were Art O'Hanlon and another member of the gang, William O'Shiel.

On the day when O'Hanlon met his death, Monday 25 April 1681, it was O'Shiel's turn to keep watch outside an abandoned cabin, where he was resting. Inside, Art sat beside him. The place was described in a pamphlet printed in Dublin in 1681, as being near 'Eight-Mile-Bridge', now Hilltown in County Down. There had been a fair at the 'Bridge', which is now known as Banbridge, and Redmond was there to intercept traders coming back and rob them.

At two o'clock in the afternoon, as Redmond lay asleep, Arthur O'Hanlon discharged his blunderbuss into Redmond's chest and then fled the scene. Lett states that when William O'Shiel heard the shot he ran into the cabin and found his leader still alive. As he lay dying, Redmond asked O'Shiel to cut off his head as soon as his 'fastly-ebbing life should be over'. This was to prevent the sport, triumph and gruesome displays of his enemies. As soon as the breath left his body, O'Shiel complied with this grim request and ran from the cabin holding his leader's head. Another source F. Mac Poilin, writing in 1936, stated that O'Shiel hid the head in a disused well close by. The decapitated body was later brought to Newry and men were sent to search for the head.

A military search party subsequently recovered the head and it was taken to Downpatrick Jail in County Down. As was the custom at the time, O'Hanlon's head was put on a spike outside the jail for all to see. Other accounts state that parts of is body were put there too, like some macabre exhibition. According to folklore, O'Hanlon's mother travelled to Downpatrick and composed a lament upon seeing her son's head spiked over the jail.

After this cowardly and treacherous deed, Art O'Hanlon received a full pardon for his previous misdemeanours and £200 from the 'Duke of Ormond' for murdering his leader. William Lucas, the planter and militia officer who had recruited Art and arranged the killing, received a lieutenant's commission in the British Army.

'Thus fell "The Irish Scanderbeg", who considering his means, and the circumstances he lay under, and the short time he continued to act, did more things to be admired than "The Scanderbeg" himself', stated Sir Francis Brewster. This 'Scanderbeg', to whom O'Hanlon is likened to, was the King of Albania, whose story reads like that of 'Jack the Giant Killer'. He was known to have cut fully armoured men in two with one swipe of his sword.

There are many stories, debates and speculation about where Redmond O'Hanlon's body found its final resting place. Revd Lett states he is buried in the parish of Ballymore in an old graveyard called Ballynaback, situated between Tandragee and Scarva, County Down. Another source states he is buried in the 'Conwal Parish Church Cemetery' in Letterkenny, County Donegal. And many believe his body is buried somewhere beneath the road from Poyntzpass to Newry in County Down. The Poyntzpass Gaelic Football team is called 'The Redmond O'Hanlons' in his honour.

There is a great belief amongst locals that the ghosts of O'Hanlon and his gang still haunt the scenes of their wild career. And tales are told of a 'Headless Ghost' roaming the lands around Hilltown in County Down.

2

THE DEMON CHIEFTAIN

This is a story I picked whilst delving deep into the annals of County Down's rich folk history. The story was sparsely recorded by a gentleman named Richard Hooke in 1891. I took it upon myself to delve a little deeper and this is what I found.

In the Mourne Mountains of County Down there is a deep and rugged valley or glen that stretches far into the centre of one section of these mountains, barren, rocky and dangerous. This valley is said to be inaccessible, its dungeon depths have never been trodden by human feet.

Out of this flows a stream of water so icy cold that it would chill you to your very soul to drink it. This stream tumbles down the rocky glen and falls into a deep lake below. Near the lake stood an ancient mound and in its centre was a cromlech consisting of four large stones surmounted with a fifth of immense size and weight. This, the legend tells, is the grave of a terrible Irish Chieftain of prehistoric times named M'Caurro. Hooke states that M'Caurro was known to have fed his 'coal-black steed' on the flesh of his slaughtered foes.

He was one of the 'Fomorians' meaning 'Under-Demons', who appeared in the twelfth-century *Irish Book of Invasions*, which contains an account of the mythical invasions of Ireland. The Fomorians were the nemesis of the Tuatha De Dannan, 'The People of the Goddess Danu', a race of divine beings said to have inhabited and ruled Ireland before the occupation of the Gaels or Celts. After the arrival of the Celts the Tuatha De Dannan relinquished their possession of the upper world and created a kingdom underground in the 'Otherworld' or 'Fairy Mounds'. This magical world was a mirror image of the upper world, but there was immortality there, agelessness and beauty and many believe they are still there, controlling the supernatural world.

On the other hand, M'Caurro's race, the Fomorians, were masters of darkness, destruction and despair. The Fomorians were defeated by the Tuatha De Dannan and those who survived the battle slowly disappeared. It seems that before he died, M'Caurro made a pact with the Devil so that he would hold some fiendish status in Hell and could return to the earth every year, on the anniversary of his death, to collect souls.

Near his grave and across the lake, in another smaller and partially wooded valley, lies the 'Devil's Well'. This well has always been regarded by the inhabitants of this lonely and sparsely populated district as a place to be avoided at all costs, for the legend states that when 'Night has donned her sable mantle' on a certain date each year, marking the anniversary of M'Caurro's death, the terrible coal-black steed of the Demon Chieftain comes trudging menacingly down the valley. He goes round the lake and up to this well, where he quenches his thirst and is joined by the Prince of Darkness and his horrid crew of servants and advisors.

From there they would repair to the chieftain's grave where some dark council and ceremony is held. One member of this diabolical council is Ignis Fatuus (foolish fire) or the 'Will-o'-the-wisp'. Both he and M'Caurro are alluded to in one of the most ancient of Irish ballads:

> The grave of the great M'Caurro
> In the Northern mountain lone
> Where the fairy thorn weeps in sorrow
> Over his mouldering stone
>
> When Lo! At the dead of midnight damp
> Is heard the bit and bridle champ
> Of the coal black steed
> And his heavy tramp
>
> Down through the valley lone
> Then the mystic sprite of the meteor lamp
> Comes gliding over the dismal swamp
> And meet by the mouldering stone.

The ballad refers to the Will-o'-the-wisp as the mystic sprite of the meteor lamp and it was said that this sprite would lead unwary travellers on the Mourne Mountains to the Devil's Well, during the hours of darkness of the Demon Chieftain's Anniversary. Travellers would see a ghostly light, resembling a flickering lamp, which would recede if they approached, drawing them from the safe paths. Many simply disappeared, others were found as corpses by the well and those who lived to tell the tale were driven mad by what they saw.

Hooke relates a sad tale concerning the well that is said to have taken place around 1810. A mile or two from the

Devil's Well lived an old widow woman with her only child in a pretty cottage. The child was said have been a delicate girl of eighteen when the old woman fell ill and died. The orphaned girl was so stricken by the sudden blow that she fell into madness. She became a wandering, though harmless, soul and was called 'Poor, Crazy Anne' by the locals.

Whether it was its wild and solitary situation or the beauty of its scenery during the day, the Devil's Well had a strange fascination for poor Anne. When the weather was mild, she would wander to the well on a daily basis. During the long summer afternoons she would sit on the edge of the well, stringing wild flowers and singing weird and melancholic songs, till the sun sank and the shades of evening gathered round, but she would always leave before darkness fell. Whether this was for the practicality of a safe footing home or a deeper awareness of something more sinister, I suppose we will never know.

Often she would tell how in the twilight, as she wept and gazed into the deep and silent waters, the lonely spirit of her dear-departed mother would appear, beckoning to her from the dim skies of a nether-world. One day the locals realised that they had not seen poor Anne for several days. A search was organised and she was finally found at her favourite haunt, the well. She was lying close by its edge, cold, stiff, discoloured and dead. She had a horrible, disfigured look of terror upon her face.

A jury, ignorant no doubt of the real facts of the case and supported by medical opinion, claimed the cause of death was an epileptic fit. But the old timers, shrewd and enlightened natives of the valley, said that the fatal night of Anne's death was that of M'Caurro's Anniversary.

Some time later one of the locals claimed to have seen 'Poor, Crazy Anne' walk in the direction of the well that fateful night (which she had never done before) and she was following what looked like a ghostly light resembling a flickering lamp, receding whenever she came too close …

To this day many walkers and hikers have disappeared or met their doom on the mountains after dark. And it is still strongly advised never to walk in the Mourne Mountains when 'Night has donned her sable mantle'.

3

AULD NICK'S HORN

I came across this wonderful tale, whilst excavating the old annals of County Down's folk history in Banbridge Library in County Down. It was recorded by an anonymous writer in 1896.

A curious custom and ceremony in connection with Midsummer's Eve in County Down took place for many years up until the turn of the last century. This custom involved decorating doorways, and sometimes even windows and chimneys, with swathes of green corn and other unripe crops. According to those who practiced these rituals, it was a process that ensured evil spirits were kept away from the premises during the succeeding twelve months. It was also believed that it helped the crops themselves flourish and yield bountiful harvests. Strangely enough, the natives of certain parts of Northern Japan had a similar practice at the same time of year. The Japanese also believed that this ritual kept malign entities from the homestead.

This custom was very common in and around Downpatrick. Some of the people liked the custom purely for its decorative aspect, whilst others took the custom seriously, hoping that it would protect them and their crops.

Within a mile or two of Downpatrick, during the mid-1800s, lived a peculiarly witch-like old crone with a wicked eye and a vicious temper. She was known as 'Kate the Thresher'. Kate was so old that she had out-lived the oldest person of the area and that is saying a good deal, as they were generally a long-living bunch in the locality. Along with her frightful temper she had a foul mouth that would make the angels weep. But her power of putting curses on people she imagined had offended her was so potent she was feared, loathed and grudgingly respected in equal measure.

Kate was well known for her exuberant and excessive adorning of her hut-like abode with vegetation. This was particularly attractive to the younger members of the community, among whom there was something of a morbid fascination about 'Kate the Thresher'.

One year she had gone to more than the usual extremities of garish decoration on her hideous hut and to finish it off she bribed a couple of young lads to climb up on the low thatched roof and suspend a beautiful wreath-like hoop adorned with all her favourite coloured flowers and vegetation around the small chimney. Of course this was a great challenge to the lads and they ran home to tell their tale of bravery behind enemy lines to their young comrades at arms. After they left, Kate sat down and looked at her adorned abode with great pride, pleasure and satisfaction until an unusually late hour. Eventually she retired to rest and slept peacefully with the knowledge she had out-done herself and her home was the safest in all the land. No evil spirit would dare come near her home if they knew what was good for them.

But poor auld Kate's rosy anticipations were shattered when a malevolent entity in the form of two mischievous young boys paid her a visit. No sooner had she gone to bed than they were hovering about her hut. In no time at all they scrambled onto her roof and quickly stripped the chimney of its much-prized hoop, replacing it with one covered in vegetation made up of rotted, ugly plants with grotesque flowers. Daylight had not long dawned the following morning, when the nearest neighbours were roused by the sound of Kate's screams of rage and disgust. As she was too old and decrepit to remove the wreath herself, she ranted at the neighbours, pleading with them to remove the offending and horrid hoop from her chimney. But the locals thought the joke far too good and refused her help. Vainly she cursed and raved and called down the most fearful threats and judgments on the heads of her tormentors. But no one would remove the wreath and ultimately, after the most trying mid-summers eve she had ever experienced in her long life, she was obliged to retire in disgust, leaving 'the banner of the foe' still in possession of her chimney. Poor auld Kate, 'shur you'd have to feel sorry for the crather'. There she was, tormented in her own home by a ring of weeds hanging round her chimney like a mill-stone hung around the neck of a drowning man.

Well you would like to think that this was the end of her persecution but the exhaustless spirit and mischievous curiosity that never seems to desert the average young boy was not yet satisfied. It was no wonder that the wee scoundrels who had carried out this successful prank, took it upon themselves to return to the scene of the crime and admire their handy work. The boys plucked up the courage to peep inside the one little window just to see what the old witch was doing and saw her sitting moodily in front of the small fireplace on which a griddle of soda bread was slowly baking. It now being dusk, the lads were full of excitement at the thought of further and bolder adventure. But the question was how to assail Kate within the walls of her own castle? One of the boys was of a particularly ingenious nature, and a bright thought at once occurred to him that a little gunpowder down Kate's chimney would present a suitable distraction. Of course no self-respecting young boy at that time was without his supply of 'villainous saltpeter'. As it happened this particular scoundrel not only had a couple of ounces of gunpowder at home, but he even had a horn (a proper cow's horn) with a plug in one end and a stopper at the other, to keep it in.

So off they hurried and soon the two conspirators returned to carry out their 'Guy Fawkes'-style attack. Kate still brooded sulkily over the fire and in a few minutes the two lads were on the roof prepared 'to give her a start'. All might have gone off innocently enough had the youngsters had the wit to take a wee bit of gunpowder in the palm of their hand and sprinkle it down the chimney. Instead of this however, one of them took the powder-horn and tipped the entire contents down the chimney spout. Immediately a huge and brilliant flame shot up from the fire below and burnt the boy's hand, causing him to let go of the horn, which fell into the chimney. There was a terrific explosion and in the ensuing confusion the conspirators managed to clear themselves from the roof-top and reach the ground below. A large crowd was already starting to assemble at the front of the house, attracted by the fireworks display and pandemonium.

To say that the boys were frightened and bemused would be an understatement to say the least. They were convinced that Kate had been killed and a hasty peep into her smoke filled abode confirmed their assessment of the situation.

The fireplace had been scattered over the small kitchen area, whilst poor auld Kate's limp, spread-eagled body lay stretched out on the floor. Nobody was in too much of a hurry to volunteer to enter the house. But eventually a couple of constables arrived at the scene. They quickly investigated the situation and carried Kate out of the smoking hovel. They were surprised to find her more frightened than injured.

In spite of all the considerations to the contrary Kate strenuously and stoutly maintained that she knew the diabolic cause of the explosion well enough. It was nothing more or less than the bodily descent of 'Auld Sootie' or 'Auld Nick', the Devil himself. She maintained that he had been attracted by his own special colours adorning the hideous hoop on her chimney. Needless to say the policemen were not too convinced with her explanation. But when they found the powder horn amongst all the chaos Kate was beside herself with jubilant defiance. 'See!' she cried, 'what did I tell yez? 'Tis wan of Auld Nick's horns!' As she appeared so satisfied, indeed pleased, with this explanation, the authorities decided to let her believe her story. They graciously allowed her to keep possession of the wondrous horn and to the day of her death she was in the habit of proudly displaying it and telling anyone who'd listen to her story about how the Devil himself had come down her chimney, attracted by the colours on the hoop that adorned it. And 'shur here was the solid proof of it: one of Auld Nick's Horn's'.

4

ST DONARD

Newcastle – the watering place of the county
With its baths at the mountains of St Donard's Wells;
Here patients resort from all ore the county
To bathe in their waters, and cull handsome shells.

(From 'A Poetical Description of Down'
by Joseph S. Adair, 1901)

Slieve Donard, Sliebh Domhanghairt, Mount Donard, has an elevation of 2,796 feet and is the highest of the Mourne Mountains in County Down. 'There are still two ruined caves on the hill, one of which was the reputed monument erected in prehistoric times to Slainge, son of Partholan, who was allegedly the first physician in Ireland, was buried there.'

The mountain is named after St Domangart or Domangard, also known as St Donard, who was a follower of St Patrick and is the patron saint of Maghera in County Down.

Domangart was the son of Eochaid, pagan King of Ulster, and his wife Derinilla. Eochaid was a wicked king, who had condemned two Christian virgins because they offered their virginity to God and they refused to marry or worship his pagan idols. He had them bound on the sea-shore and left, helpless against the incoming tide, to drown under the merciless waves.

Patrick had begged the king to pardon them so that they should not be punished, but it was not granted. The king's brother Cairell attempted to negotiate with the king, but to no avail. Patrick, in his rage and disgust, laid a curse on Eochaid, saying, 'There will never be either kings or crown-princes from thee …', predicting instead that the king's brother Cairell and his sons would rule over all Ulster. The king's wife Derinilla was hurt by this curse and its effect on her unborn child. So she went and laid herself at Patrick's feet, begging for mercy as she had no part in the murder of the two girls. Patrick gave her a blessing, and blessed the unborn boy-child in her womb, that he should have the grace of God protect him; the boy was named Domangart or Donard.

Canon H.W. Lett, writing in 1905, states that Donard grew to be fine young man and was a great hunter and warrior. One day he came across a holy man wandering his land whilst on one of his hunting expeditions. Now Donard had a magnificent bull, which he was terribly proud of (at that time in Ireland to possess a strong, virile and fierce bull was a symbol of great wealth and power). The bull charged at the holy man, roaring and tearing up the earth below him as he ploughed towards the trespasser.

But the stranger held up the staff he was holding and pointed it towards the charging bull. As soon as he did this the beast was torn to pieces before Donard's eyes. In disbelief Donard dismounted his horse and, in his grief and apparent madness, tried to gather up the pieces of the dismembered animal and place them together again. He begged the stranger to restore the bull to its former life and ferocity. The stranger waved his great staff and Donard watched in amazement as the all the organs, flesh, bones and skin of the beast were restored to their original functions and the bull started into life with all its original fierceness.

At the sight of this Donard was seized with dismay, and throwing himself at the feet of the holy man, begged that he would take him under his protection and make him one of his people or sacred household by baptising him. This stranger was none other than St Patrick. From this moment onwards Donard became a meek and humble disciple. He gave up his lands, wealth and fortified residence. No more did he engage in hunting elk and other wild beasts of the plain. Instead, he took to fasting and praying and learning the gospels and holy texts. He lived as a hermit on the mountain Slieve Slangra (now called 'Slieve Donard' after him) and built a cell or oratory on top of it. It was said that Donard's mother had four breasts and these are represented by the four hills surrounding the highest peak on Slieve Donard.

Donard feast day is 24 March and his church was named 'Rath Muirbuilc', now called 'Maghera', and lay inland from Newcastle, where the stump of a round tower and a medieval church still marks the early site.

His death is given as AD 507, but according to the book *Tripartite* St Donard was among the immortalised seven men that St Patrick chose from his sacred household, or *familia*, to safeguard Ireland and who are all still alive today.

There was a tradition at Easter to bring a meal of mutton and beer to Maghera for St Donard and this became the 'Feast of Mutton' that took place every Easter Monday.

It was said St Donard was bestowed with a very special and important duty to perform: it was his business to guard St Patrick's relics from harm until the 'Day of Doom'. Whether he still lives or when the Day of Doom nears nobody knows, but the majestic beauty of Slieve Donard remains, towering above the Mountains of Mourne to this very day in County Down.

St Patrick, Ireland's patron saint, is universally remembered and revered as the man who brought Christianity to Ireland in the fifth century. When he was a youth he lived in Wales but was kidnapped and taken to Ireland to be sold into slavery by the pirate 'Niall of the Nine Hostages'. He was already a Christian before being sold into slavery but his faith grew in captivity (near Slemish in mid-Antrim). After six years working as a shepherd he finally escaped by boat to France and made his way home to Wales. It was there that he was visited by the angel, Victor, and told to return to Ireland, to spread the word of Christianity. He did return and spent the rest of his life preaching the gospel in Ireland.

Muirchú's seventh-century 'Life of Saint Patrick' describes Patrick's work in County Down. Muirchú tells how Patrick landed at Inber Slane (identifiable with a river called the Slaney) and converted the local chief, Díchu, who lived 'where Patrick's barn is now'. Díchu gave Patrick his barn to use as a church. He returned to Lecale and 'favoured and loved the district, and the faith began to spread there'. When close to death, he was told by the angel Victor to 'return to the place from which you came, that is, to Sabul', where he died. By the seventh century the whereabouts of Patrick's burial were disputed. Muirchú's account states firmly that Downpatrick in County Down is where Patrick lies buried.

5

THE GILLHALL GHOST

Gillhall lies a mile or so outside of Dromore in County Down, and it was here that this spectral tale of ghosts and curses took place.

The Beresfords have been so long associated with County Waterford that few people apart from professional genealogists remember their long and intimate association with Ulster. The Beresfords originated from Boresford, in Staffordshire, England, and the first apparently to enter Ireland was Sir Tristram Beresford, who settled in Coleraine as manager of the 'Society of the New Plantation in Ulster'. The family took root. Money and honours were gathered. At a time when the family were lucky to be on the winning side in the wars with King James II, a great-grandson of Sir Tristram Beresford, another Tristram, came of age. In 1687 he married Nicola Sophia Hamilton and it is she who is the central character of this story.

Nicola Hamilton was orphaned at an early age and was raised, along with her cousin John Le Peor, on the Gillhall estate in Dromore, County Down. As children Nicola and her cousin formed an unusual pact; unsure of what was waiting for them in the afterlife and if there was any real God, they decided to make a bargain with each other that whoever was to die first should return to the other and enlighten the remaining one as to what was on the other side.

After their marriage, every Autumn Sir Tristram and Lady Beresford would pay a visit to her sister Lady Macgill, who still lived in the townland of Gillhall and it was on one of their visits, in October 1693, that something truly terrifying happened. On Halloween night Lady Nicola was visited by her cousin, John Le Peor. But this was not a casual seasonal drop in. He was hovering above her bed, transparent and terrifying. She was frozen with fear as he moved like a shadow, floating towards her. He had come to fulfil his side of their childhood pact and to tell her of what lay beyond the grave and what the future held for her and those close to her.

He told her he had died three days ago and that her husband Tristram would die within four years. She would remarry, but it would be to a wastrel and they would separate, but eventually be reconciled. Lastly he told of her own death; she would die and join him on her forty-seventh birthday.

Poor Nicola could not believe what was happening and asked that he show her some sign of his existence and that this was not all a terrible nightmare. With that he grabbed her by the wrist and a terrible burning sensation ran through her arm. She screamed with both terror and pain. Amazingly no one heard her nor came to her aid. She was alone scared and confused. The ghost of John tore his hand away from her aching wrist leaving a burn mark, like it had been scalded. He also slammed his fiery hand against the wardrobe, leaving a scorched hand print upon it. She collapsed and fainted, falling into a welcome world of oblivion free from all this torment and anxiety.

When she came to the next morning, she shuddered as she recalled the terrible nightmare she had the night before. Then she looked at her wrist and there was the awful burn mark. It had not been a dream. Her wrist no longer hurt, but it felt cold like ice. Frightened and confused, she hid the injury on her wrist under a length of black ribbon and hurried down to breakfast.

When Lady Beresford appeared at breakfast her husband noticed that she seemed very frightened and confused and looked extremely pale, but she assured her anxious husband she was well. He noticed that her wrist was bound with a black ribbon. 'Have you hurt your wrist?' he asked.

'No,' she replied, 'No I have not but pray never ask me about this band, and never urge me further on the subject.'

She then asked twice had the post arrived. 'Are you expecting any letters?' asked Sir Tristram, concerned and bemused.

'I am,' she cried. 'I expect to hear that Lord Tyrone is dead, he died last Tuesday at four o'clock'.

Tristram could not understand what his wife was talking about, but at that moment the door opened and a servant handed in a letter sealed with black wax. It was from Tyrone's steward and it stated that his master had died on Tuesday last at the hour of four o'clock.

Sir Tristram could see that Lady Nicola was genuinely disturbed, and asked her what had upset her so much and how she had known that her cousin had died. She told him of the nocturnal visit of Lord Tyrone and of some of the things he had related to her. Then a change came over her and she seemed to become more at ease as she told her husband that her cousin had told her they would have a son together.

In the following year, 1694, the promised son was born and several years after that Sir Tristram died. After his death, the widow lived a very secluded life, as if she was hiding from something. She seldom left the house and she did not entertain guests for fear she may be inviting death into her home. The only people she did visit were the family of the local parish clergyman. This clergyman had a son, 'Young Gorges', and it was to him that Lady Nicola was eventually married, in 1704.

Gorges was not a very nice man and was keen to partake in the extra-curriculum activities of army life. He had many affairs and took little interest in his new wife, other than her wealth. Poor Nicola had two daughters with Gorges and, fearing for his influence on the young girls, Lady Nicola separated from him for several years. But, just as Lord Tyrone had predicted that Halloween night, she eventually pardoned Gorges and once more resided with him. She then had a son with him.

Exactly a month to the day after her second son was born it was her forty-seventh birthday. It descended on her like a great menacing shadow. She did not know what to expect but she was certainly full of fear and anticipation. What a relief it was to her when her birthday passed without any drama. So the following year of 1713 Lady Nicola threw a huge masked ball to celebrate her forty-eighth birthday, her defiance of death and also proving her cousin wrong in his fortune telling.

During the night Lady Nicola, who was wearing a skull mask as a sign of her defiance, was approached by the clergyman who had baptised her. He wished her a happy forty-seventh birthday. She corrected him, telling the old man that it was her forty-eighth, and he of all people should know that. But he pointed out to her that she was born in 1666 and not 1667 and offered to show her the birth records for that year. Nicola was horrified and was said to have told the old vicar, 'You have signed my death warrant. I have not much longer to live. I entreat you all to leave immediately, and send for my children, as I have something of grave importance to settle before I die.'

The startled children accordingly went to their mother who, after taking a deep breath, began her story. 'I have something of importance to communicate to you, my sweet children, before I must go.' She told her children of the Lord Tyrone apparition and his prophecy of her death and she revealed her wrist; even after all these years it was still shrunken and withered as if burnt in a terrible fire.

The poor children, confused and frightened, were taken from her on her own request and she ordered the attendants to wait outside the room and only to come if called. An hour passed in silence and then they heard the sound of the most terrible screaming and shrieking coming from her room. They flew to her aid only to find her lying sprawled out on the bed with the most horrific expression of fear distorting her face and her eyes bulging from their sockets. The black ribbon had fallen from her wrist and the rest of her body bore the same terrible scar tissue that marked her wrist. It was as if she had been burnt alive but there were no signs of fire damage anywhere else in the room.

Her body was taken to St Patrick's Cathedral in Dublin, where she was laid to rest. There is a portrait of her with the bound-up wrist in Howth Castle, County Dublin, but the black ribbon was later taken out of the picture as it was considered to be bad luck.

Gillhall House lay empty for many years. It was briefly reoccupied by the Royal Air Force during the Second World War but then lay empty again. The house was burnt down in June of 1969 and now its empty shell still stands, like a yawning skull, overlooking the County Down countryside, a watchful spectre waiting for unwary visitors to enter its echoing chambers.

6

THE CON-MAN

This is a wee folk story that was told by Dan Rooney of Lurgancanty; a small townland in County Down that lies quietly between Warrenpoint and Mayobridge in the parish of Clonallon. Rooney was a farmer who also worked as a cart driver on the side, to make ends meet. He had a great singing voice and was a keen huntsman, renowned for hunting hares. According to Michael J. Murphy, who was a keen and respected collector of Irish folklore, Dan Rooney was the last of the great storytellers of County Down. He states, 'As far as I can ascertain from enquiry and personal knowledge, Dan Rooney was one of the very last (if not indeed the last) of the real folk Storytellers within the terrain of the Mournes'. Rooney lived all his life in Lurgancanty and died there in 1962, at the age eighty-one. This particular story is one that Murphy seemed to have a lot of affection for so I have put it in this collection of County Down folk tales, with my own twist on it.

Well there was once a man who did not have a whole lot in this world during a time when many had nothing at all.

In regard to this fact he happened to have much more than others around him when it came to wit and wiliness. But for his abundance of craftiness he had little compassion or regard for his fellow man. This particular man was from Lurgancanty in the County of Down and one day he took it upon himself to go to Newry, in the same County, to buy some corn. As was mentioned before he had more than others and one of the possessions that confirmed this fact was his ownership of a horse. Now although he had a horse he had no pockets or bag to put his money in. So he stored it under the straw matting that served as a saddle on his steed.

When he got to Newry, he tied his horse up in a stable and gave it some hay and water to sate its appetite after such a long journey. Now the straw mats with the money held in them he placed on a ledge near the beast.

He then made his way to the market and bought a bag of corn. As he had no money on him, due to the lack of a vessel to carry it in, he returned to the stable with the corn merchant, intending to extract the correct amount of money from the straw mats in order to pay the man. But lo and behold when he got back, the horse had not only eaten all the hay but also the straw mats with the money in them. And there it was the whole lot, 'Gone!' The money was all in sovereigns and half-sovereigns, and there was a fair amount indeed. Well there was nothing else for it he had to wait for the horse to 'dung'. And there he stood beside his horse and he waited and waited. When eventually the horse did go to the toilet he started hoking around in the horse dung finding first one coin and then another and carefully put them to one side. Whilst this was all going on the man whom he had bought the corn from was standing by, watching and waiting to be paid.

Well the man watching all this carry on was very impressed with this horse that could pass money through its backside. He approached the man and said he had never seen such a thing. He asked him if the horse did this all the time and the other man, sensing a money-making opportunity, said it did. He told him the more you fed the horse the more money came out the other end. 'By God,' said the corn merchant, 'will ya sell him to me?'

'I will,' replied the other. And sell the horse he did for a very fine price too.

When the corn merchant got home he told his wife about this magic horse that he had bought from a fella he was selling corn to at the market in Newry. Of course, she was very suspicious about the dubious deal. The man gave her a demonstration and needless to say there was no money to be found in the horse's dung, not a penny. 'I'll get me money back!' cried the man, angry at being tricked and being made a fool of.

Now in the meantime the cunning Lurgancanty man knew fine rightly that his dupe would be coming looking for his money. So he told his wife of this and handed her a stone. Now at this time she had a big pot of stew on the boil over the fire and her husband told her to take the stew off the crook and when the other man arrived she was to put it back on, but instead of heaping the fire underneath it she was just to put the stone below it, letting-on that this was what was heating the stew. His wife was not at all happy with his plan but he warned her that if she was to make a mistake or not do as he asked there would be hell to pay. With that he headed off, leaving his poor frightened wife behind. Not long after the other man arrived, furious and looking for the trickster.

'Calm down and have some stew,' said the woman 'he is out and about.' She lifted the stew pot from the floor and put it on the crook, picked up the stone and put it below it. Within a minute the pot was bubbling away and the woman tasted it.

'Ahh, 'tis ready' she said.

'What a great stone that is,' remarked the man.

'Oh! It saves me plenty on coals,' replied the woman. Totally distracted by this the man blurted out, 'Can I buy it off ya?'

The woman wholeheartedly agreed and the poor man left with less money that he had come with and a useless auld stone.

Ah! Dear sweet mother divine, when the poor fellow got home only to realise he had been tricked again, he was beside himself in grief at being such a fool. He swore to his poor wife that he would get the money back. She looked at her husband and said she would get the money back herself but he would have none of it. As far as he was concerned, it was his blunder and he should rectify it. So off he went to get his money, the poor unfortunate fool that he was.

His wife watched him as he left and her mind went to work, thinking of the trickster and what she might do if her poor husband was humiliated again. He may not have had the biggest intellect but he had a heart a big as a mountain and she loved him dearly.

In the meantime the trickster was back at his own house and he had to think of another plan to deter this fool of a man who was on his way for his money. Now this cunning devil happened to have two hares in a cage at the back of his house. He told his wife what he wanted her to do and to do it right. When the fool came to look for his money she was to tell him that her husband was away down by the shore, three miles away. She would then send one of the hares to look for him and bring him home. The poor wife thought this was such an outrageous scheme that not even a fool would fall for it but her husband shouted at her to mind her own business and keep her opinions to herself if she knew what was good for her. 'If you shout or whistle or blow a horn or anything,' says he, 'I'll have yer bleddy life!'

So off he went again, leaving his dutiful wife to do his dirty work. It wasn't long before the other man arrived. He asked her where her husband was and she explained that he was away off down by the shore. But she had a well-trained hare that would go down to the beach and take him a message to return home. So she went and got one of the hares from the cage and made a show of patting the animal gently on the head and whispering something in its ear. She let go of the hare and off he ran, like the wind, down towards the shore below.

When the trickster saw the hare run past him he knew it was time to start making his way back. Sure enough, when he returned home, the man was there waiting for him. 'Well now!' says the man, bemused by what he saw. 'That's a great hare.'

'He's far better and quicker than any servant boy for takin' a message' replied the trickster.

'Would you sell me that hare?' asked the man.

Of course the con-man agreed straight away and said that he would go and get the hare as it was out the back in its usual place. He went to the back of the house and took the other hare from the cage and brought it to the man and fetched a fine price for it.

Well the man went home with the hare but as soon as he let go of it, it darted off across the fields, never to be seen again. He fell to his knees and wept like a child, berating himself for being so foolish. It was then that his wife appeared and she consoled her poor husband who apologised to her for being so foolish and naive.

'Ah! Not to worry my dear,' she said, comforting her husband. 'I think I know of a way to make all this right'. She told her husband to listen very carefully and do exactly as she asked. He was all ears for even he knew that he was beat and any further action under his own self-will and direction would only lead to more disaster.

She told him to go around to the trickster's house and be as happy and jovial as he could be. When asked why he was so happy he was to tell his nemesis that he had been to Heaven. And when asked how, he was to take the con-man back home and she would take care of the rest.

Well he did exactly as he was told and headed off to the man's house, singing and skipping all the way like a man who hadn't a care in the world. When he arrived the trickster had already another plan up his sleeve to fool his victim with. But he was surprised to see how happy he was and even more surprised when he was told by the man that there was no more bad blood between the two of them and he could keep his money; 'Shur there's no need for money where I have been' he says.

'And where might that be now?' asked the con-man. 'Shur' I've been to Heaven and back' he says. "Tis a fine place, where a fella wouldn't have any worry or trouble at all'. Of course, this whetted the con-man's appetite to find out more. 'So where is Heaven then?' he asked. 'Come back to my house and I'll show you'. The con-man's wife was curious too and asked could she come as well. 'Of course,' replied the man. 'Mind you only one at a time can get into Heaven, the entrance is very small'.

'She'll not be going to Heaven,' roared the con-man. 'I'll make sure of that'. So they all headed off together.

When they arrived back at the house, the other man's wife was there to greet them. 'So where is this doorway to Heaven then?' cried the con-man. The woman was holding a sack and explained that heaven was in the bag. The con-man laughed out loud at this. The woman explained that she had asked her husband to take the last few spuds from the sack for the dinner and when he put his head down into to get a good look, he disappeared and came back with money and bread. 'I'll show you,' said her husband. He crawled inside the bag and returned with coins and bread, which were already in the bag.

Well, the con-man didn't believe that such a fool could come up with such a story, so it must be true. Without a second wasted, he climbed into the bag, as soon as he did the other man grabbed the end and his wife tied a piece of rope around it, making sure that he could not escape. He kicked and roared and screamed and cursed them all to hell. 'And that's where you belong!' cried the woman. He called out to his own wife and swore if she didn't let him out he would kill her and she knew that even if she did he would do it anyway, but she was having none of it, pleased at the fate that had befallen her brute of a husband. They dragged the sack to edge of the cliff and threw it over. And, as Dan Rooney said, 'An, that was the last of him'.

7

SQUIRE HAWKINS

This is a great wee story that I was given by a well-known local librarian from County Down. It is one of those stories that remind us of the libertines and rascals that are so often censored from history books. This man, like the libertine Lord Byron, was indeed 'Mad, Bad and Dangerous to Know'. He was called William Hawkins, also known as Squire Hawkins. Squire Hawkins' body lies in a grave near the old Drumballyroney Church in County Down. This is also where Patrick Brontë, the father of the elusive Brontë sisters, taught as a school master at the school-house there.

William Hawkins was Alderman to King Charles II. He had supposedly clothed and fed the king's armies and as reward for his services he acquired the land lost to the McGennis clan, the Irish chieftains who had ruled over the barony of Iveagh from the twelfth to the seventeenth centuries from their castle on the hill at Rathfriland.

Local folklore states that the ghost of the last Lord Iveagh still relentlessly paces up and down the only remaining wall of his stronghold on Castle Hill, with his hands thrust deep in his pockets, trying to hold on to his last bit of land and fortune.

As soon as William Hawkins acquired the land including the castle, he immediately proceeded to dismantle the MaGennis castle stone by stone and used the materials to build the Clanwilliam Arms in the square of Rathfriland. He was reputedly one of the founder members of Rathfriland's Hellfire Club. He and the rest of the members of this ill-reputed club met in the cellars of the Clanwilliam Arms. The Hellfire Club was a name for several exclusive clubs for high-society libertines established in Britain and Ireland in the seventeenth and eighteenth centuries, and was more formally or cautiously known as the Order of the Friars of St Francis of Wycombe.

Not much is known about the goings on of the Hellfire Club – there were rumours relating that the members met there to worship the Devil – but one can be sure that there was a great deal of debauchery, devilment and drinking and it certainly was not a club for the faint-hearted. There was also a Hellfire Club in Dublin on Montpelier Hill; this was a hunting lodge built around 1725 by a William Connolly and it was renowned for its blasphemous orgies, black masses and demonic manifestations. Apparently 'Auld Nick' himself made a couple of guest appearances there.

The bad reputation of Squire Hawkins and his Hellfire Club did not comply with the beliefs of the God-fearing and clean-living local people of Rathfriland. But he was so greatly feared by the people that he had no problem exercising his authority over those who dared oppose him and his ways. He was as cruel as he was villainous and took great delight in the suffering and humiliation of others, especially those who did not recognise his lord and master Satan as the all-powerful force who ruled everything.

Squire Hawkins was the wealthiest man in Rathfriland and when he died in 1680 there was an elaborate funeral held for him. Of course, none of the locals attended nor were they invited. One can assume it was a dark and unholy affair. Nevertheless his black coffin was carried on the back of a great hearse drawn by two huge black-plumed horses with his family and servants walking behind it to the graveyard at Drumballyroney. It is a wonder that such a character would be allowed to be buried in hallowed ground but it proved the authority and power he had over the people even in death.

It is said that when the hearse approached the gates of the graveyard, the black horses reared up, foaming at the mouth and refused to enter into the graveyard. They were completely terrified and their whinnies and snorts could be heard all around. No matter how much they were whipped and pushed and pulled, this way and that, nothing could get them to go through the gates. In the end Squire Hawkins' coffin had to be lifted from the hearse and carried to the grave, where it was lowered into the ground and covered with soil. They say that at that moment the sky filled with dark clouds and thunder and lightning lit up the land. The locals all ran to their homes and locked their doors and prayed for protection.

The most ferocious thunderstorm the town of Rathfriland had ever witnessed roared through the night like an army of angry demons rampaging through the skies above. The locals said it was the Devil and his horrid crew coming from Hell to claim Squire Hawkins' soul.

The next day a few of the family members thought they should go and check on the grave to make sure it was alright after the thunderstorm. What they saw they found hard to

believe. Sometime during the thunderstorm the tombstone had been struck by lightning and split in four. The lines on the broken tombstone made the sign of the cross.

Everyone in Rathfriland claimed it was God's way of getting his revenge on Squire Hawkins who didn't believe in him. The graveyard where he is buried is said to be haunted, with many reports of strange and ghostly apparitions. Several paranormal researchers have carried out various investigations at the Drumballyroney Church and School House there. There is also a mass grave of people slaughtered at a battle that took place during the great Ulster Plantation against Oliver Cromwell's Roundheads. This grave is a strange balance between the romantic and the macabre. People often go there to be married due to its romantic connection with the Brontës. But make sure if you decide to tie the knot there that you steer well clear of the grave of Squire Hawkins otherwise the blessing may not be what you had planned or bargained for.

8

THE HAUNTED BRIDGE

This is a wee gem collected by the Revd J.B. Lusk of Glascar in 1924. The story itself takes place in the early 1800s and is a real spine-chiller with a dark-humour all of its own. So please settle in for the terrifying tale of Bonnety's Bridge.

Bonnety's Bridge is an ancient high-arched stone bridge on the old road from Rathfriland to Poyntzpass. It lies about seven and a half miles from Newry, four from Rathfriland and six from Banbridge, all of which are in County Down.

And where or from whom did this bridge get its unusual and innocuous name from? Some say that 'Bonnety' was derived from an old Irish word meaning 'The Rushy Bottom' or 'The Feeding Place of the Pigs'. Another explanation was that it was connected with the 'B Specials', as it was a favourite meeting place of theirs, and its name derived from the peculiar shape of the caps they wore. However, I am about to tell you the true account of the origin of the name 'Bonnety's Bridge', I hope you are sitting comfortably.

The bridge was always considered to be a place to be avoided after dark, and the local people, and anyone who knew about it, made long detours to avoid crossing it at night. You see, the bridge was believed to be haunted by a cruel-looking old woman all dressed in black mourning garb and sporting an immense black bonnet. It was due to this huge headdress that 'Bonnety' got her name. Apparently if a traveller or travellers approached the bridge the old woman would come from the other side to meet them, hissing like an angry swan and then, with lightning speed, vault over their heads, landing behind them, laughing hysterically and chattering incomprehensible incantations. The old woman would then jump from the bridge, shrieking and hissing, and run under one of the arches like a giant black water hen. As the travellers attempted to continue crossing the bridge to the old gate on the other side, they could hear the old woman counting out each of their steps with this hideous rhyme:

> One, two I can hear and see you
> Three, four I'm under the floor
> Five, six I'll snap your bones like sticks
> Seven, eight will you make to the gate?
> Nine, ten don't ever come here again!

Of course, once these poor souls did make it to the gate, they ran for their lives and never did come back again.

So the question is, who was 'Bonnety'? Some say she was a woman crazed with grief or crossed in love who drowned herself. Others say she was a cruel widowed mother who was eventually killed by a relative who threw her from the bridge in order to protect the children. Whatever the

reasons for her death she was compelled to re-visit the bridge and no mortal would dare return to it once they had encountered 'Bonnety'.

There are lots of stories that surround the bridge and its phantom sentinel. But there is one in particular that stands out. Not content with frightening belated travellers, the old woman proceeded to further atrocities. Glascar Mill at the time was a humble structure owned by a bachelor who lived in a two-roomed house beside the mill, about 200 yards from the bridge. Late one night, or early one morning, he happened to awake without any apparent cause and was wide awake at that. He later recalled, 'I sat up in me bed fellin' a bit quare'. He climbed out of bed, opened the door between the bedroom and kitchen and saw, by the dim light of the raked-up turf fire, an old woman in a huge bonnet hunkered down over the ashes. He slowly backed towards the bedroom, barred the door, jumped into his bed and covered his head with the sheets. But he soon discovered that a barred door was no obstacle for a disembodied spirit, for no sooner was he completely covered like a rabbit in his burrow, the bonneted beast landed without a sound on top of the bedclothes. The sheer terror of this so overcame the poor man that he lost consciousness.

When he came to, he felt himself being pinned down onto the bed as if a millstone had been laid on the bedclothes above him. He could hear the woman breathing and muttering words but they made no sense to him whatsoever. Her body was ice cold and made a cracking noise when it shifted disjointedly on top of him. With the discomfort, fear and sheer weirdness of the situation, the bachelor lay paralysed till the dawn compelled the woman to leave as noiselessly as she came.

At this point of the story there are various versions, according to Lusk, as to what happened next. Some have it that immediate steps were taken to destroy the phantom, but Lusk suggests that this is unlikely as the locals were never much given to raw haste. 'Slow but sure' was always their motto, explains Lusk, with the emphasis on the slow. They maintained that the less sure you are the slower you ought to go and this was definitely a situation riddled with uncertainty. Lusk states that his best source for the outcome of this paranormal performance was a local old man in his late nineties whom he had met during the 1890s. According to this old-timer the bachelor gradually came to terms with his traumatic experience.

Time passed and 'Bonnety' was not mentioned again; the people had evidently decided that the threat was gone and by not talking about her, her existence was dissipated. But still no one went near the bridge after dark; this was an unspoken rule, strictly adhered to. That is, until one night, when a couple of travellers, ignorant of the danger, crossed the bridge and were soon seen shouting and screaming about 'Horrid shapes and shrieks and sights unholy!' After this nobody could sleep at night and nobody would go out at night unless in company. 'Bonnety' was at large again and it was agreed that it was high time something was done.

To this end, a Presbyterian minister was consulted. He was appalled at these fanciful Godless superstitions and condemned the people as heathen blasphemers. So there was only one thing for it and, according to Lusk, 'this shows the desperation of the people', they were compelled to seek the aid of a Roman Catholic priest. He professed himself willing and able to deal with a whole legion of spirits but when he arrived at the Mill House he said that a grave moral

dilemma presented itself to him. He could easily drive the old woman from their borders and make her impotent to trouble them, but there were other bridges and other lone bachelors in the world besides those in Glascar. In other townlands people sometimes walked late at night. Who knew where she might take herself when she was driven out, or what harm she might do. It would be an act of fiendish cruelty to let her loose on the world at large, enraged as she undoubtedly would be by her enforced departure from her rightful place. However, he also claimed that he had a solution. In order that she might be properly cabined, cribbed and confined, he proposed to cork her up in a bottle and bury her!

There might be some trouble inducing her to enter a bottle, but the old padre had thought of that too. It was a well-known fact to those who are accustomed to dealing with demons and ghosts that they will easily be enticed into any place where there had never been anything but pure spirits. He therefore demanded a full bottle of whiskey and a good cork, so there would be no danger of any contamination. When asked what size of bottle he required he replied he needed, 'A good big wan, so there'd be plenty a room for her, a quart should do da trick!' The bottle and cork were brought hastily; nobody suggested that the whiskey should be poured into the mill race to make room for the demon. The priest made sure to dispose of it in a very non-wasteful fashion and also guaranteed the new vessel was blessed. When the bottle was empty he told the crowd to stay in their homes and he would go out and deal with the ghost.

What spell or incantation he used nobody knows, but after a considerable interval they heard a terrible whooping, hollering and then low groaning, finally followed a loud 'Whoop! Ya boy ya!' The priest then came in and triumphantly announced that he had Bonnety corked in the bottle. Bonnety was safely bottled up and it would be dangerous for them to let her loose again. The priest said that the bottle must be buried at the bridge and then he would bless the bridge so that there would be no further disturbances at Bonnety's final resting place. The priest seemed to be bearing an awful weight in the bottle as he went to bridge, so much that he almost missed his footing at times, but he held onto the bottle for dear life. He made the people dig a hole about two feet deep below one of the bridge-arches and in it he placed the bottle. It was said that no water ever ran through that arch afterwards.

There the bottle stayed for a long time but there was a great flood in 1915 and the bottle was supposed to have been dredged up from its grave. Whether it was washed out to sea, lodged itself in another field or found its home on top of someone's mantelpiece we will never know. But somewhere out there is a quart-sized bottle with a good strong cork and may the powers that be, help and protect the poor soul unfortunate enough to find it and to dare open it, for curiosity can often cost far more than one bargained for.

9

FRANCIS CROZIER AND THE SEARCH FOR THE NORTH-WEST PASSAGE

I came across this little gem from 1927 in the annals of Banbridge Library about the doomed expedition of Francis Crozier and his quest to find the North-West Passage. There is a statue of Captain Francis Crozier in Banbridge, County Down. There he stands tall and proud, surrounded by polar bears (said by many to resemble cocker spaniels).

In 1927 the Banbridge Household Almanac received a copy of the Toronto Star Weekly from an old Banbridge man, Mr Robert Duff, announcing that a Canadian explorer was on his way to discover, if possible, more information of the tragedy which overtook Captain Crozier of Banbridge, Sir John Franklin, and the crew which set out some eighty-two years earlier on their fatal voyage to discover the Canadian Arctic. The story is both fascinating and tragic.

Bound for those desolate wastes of the world's ice cap, into those grim regions where death overtook Sir John Franklin and the 129 members of his expedition of 1845 and later, a Canadian explorer is now in the north on a lone patrol to seek further data on the tragedy which eighty-two years ago shocked all Britain.

Where Sir John Franklin and some of the ablest naval officers of the day fought their way in with the *Erebus* and the *Terror*, Major L.S. Burwash, son of a former chancellor of Victoria University will sail in a cockle-shell of a schooner with only an Eskimo crew to aid him. Into Victoria Strait, where two of the stoutest ships of the old British navy were locked in a death grip of winter ice, Major Burwash plans to sail his little *Ptarmigan* before many months have passed.

Toronto Star Weekly

This was just the latest of several expeditions that Burwash had made in his efforts to discover just what had happened to Sir John Franklin and his crew.

Sir John Franklin was a famed Arctic explorer, having successfully led several expeditions in the area. In 1845 he had set sail in search of the fabled North-West Passage. He had two ships, the *Erebus* and the *Terror*, under his command and 129 men. The last sighting of the ships was on 26 July, after which nothing was heard or seen of them. They had simply vanished.

Lady Franklin, who never gave up hope that her husband might still be alive, persuaded the Admiralty to send out rescue expeditions. In six years twenty-one relief parties set sail, 21,000 miles of Arctic shore line were explored in the search for Franklin and, bit by bit, evidence was found that pieced together what had happened on that fateful voyage.

It was Captain Penny, master of the *Lady Franklin*, sailing under Admiralty orders and following the course laid down for Franklin, who finally came to Beechey Island. The ruins of Franklin's camp were still there suggesting that the expedition had over-wintered there in 1845. More worryingly, 600 empty cans which had contained the specially prepared meat taken by Franklin were found on the island. After the expedition had sailed the Admiralty had discovered that the meat of this issue had deteriorated and the find of 600 empty tins on Beechey Island suggested that the expedition had found a large portion of its food supply was useless and had been forced to discard it.

It was the search for the North-West Passage which cost Franklin his life and, ironically, it was in searching for Franklin and his men that the discovery was made that there actually was such a passage. As part of the search, Captain McClure was sent round the Horn in the *Investigator*, accompanied by Captain Collinson in another ship. He became separated from Collinson after entering the Arctic seas from the Pacific and for three years no word came from him and he was given up for lost. Then, in the fourth year he reappeared, but on the other side. He had been forced to abandon his ship off Melville Island. With his supplies giving out and his crew wracked by exposure and privation, he made his way across the ice and reached another search party commanded by Sir Edward Belcher. He had proved that there was a North-West Passage.

Nothing further, however, was found of Franklin and his voyage. Years later, when all hope of finding Franklin alive had been abandoned, Lady Franklin, hearing of an American expedition in 1885 going into the Arctic, ordered that a marble tablet be erected to the memory of her husband and to the men who died in the expedition. This was carved in New York, there being no time to send one out from England, and the captain was asked to take it to Beechey Island. The tablet reached Godhaven, in

Greenland, and was left there, the American expedition not going on to Beechey.

The devoted widow spent her all in the unavailing search for her husband. The last of her fortune went in outfitting the yacht *Fox*, commanded by Captain McClintock, who, touched by the grief of Lady Franklin, gave his services gratuitously in a last effort to find trace of the missing men.

When passing Godhaven, Captain McClintock picked up the memorial tablet and when he reached Beechey Island he erected it to the memory of Franklin, for this was before he discovered the real place of Franklin's death. In the library of the North-West Territories branch at Ottawa is a copy of McClintock's record of his voyage, in which he tells of the placing of the memorial.

> I placed it upon a raised, flagged square in the centre of which is recorded the names of those who perished in the Government expedition under Sir Edward Belcher. Here also is placed a tablet to the memory of Lieutenant Bellot. I could not have selected for Lady Franklin's memorial a more appropriate and conspicuous site.
>
> The inscription runs as follows: 'To the memory of Franklin, Crozier, FitzJames and all their gallant brother officers and faithful companions who have suffered and perished in the cause of science and the service of their country. This tablet is erected near the spot where they passed their first Arctic winter and whence they issued forth to conquer difficulties or to die. It commemorates the grief of their admiring countrymen and friends and the anguish, subdued by faith of her who has lost, in the heroic leader of the expedition, the most devoted and affectionate of husbands. "And so he bringeth them into the haven where they would be." 1855.'

Captain J.E. Bernier, a Canadian explorer, visited the memorial on one of his northern trips and in the *Cruise of the Arctic* he says:

> We decided to build a cement foundation for this tablet which was flat on the stone sills. We landed three-fourths of the crew with six barrels of cement. We set the tablet in this cement in an upright position. We also painted the headstone that had been erected at that place in memory of three men, members of the crew of the *Erebus* and the *Terror*.

The climax of McClintock's search came when he got to Boothia Peninsula and continued their expedition by dog sledge. Finally they met with four Eskimos. On the garb of one was a naval button. It came, they said, from some white people who were starved on an island. The Eskimos also produced some iron knives which came from the same place. None of them had seen the white men. McClintock hired the Eskimos to build a hut, paying them one needle each. An Eskimo woman importunately demanded a needle and McClintock records that, 'she plucked her baby by the arm out of the fur bag on her back and held it there naked with the temperature 60 below zero, begging a needle for the baby.'

By this time McClintock and his men were bartering with the Eskimos for the silver spoons and forks of the Franklin expedition which had come into their possession. Later they bartered with other Eskimos for pieces of silver plate with the crest of Franklin or his captains, Crozier and FitzJames, paying from two to four needles for each piece. They found an old woman and a boy who had actually seen one of the vessels when it was sunk, probably when the Eskimos down in the hold, chopped a hole in the side to let in the light, but chopped below the waterline and sank the boat.

'She said many of the white men dropped by the way as they went to the Great River, that some were buried and some were not; they did not witness this but discovered their bodies during the winter following,' records McClintock.

On 24 May they found the skeleton of a young man who had 'dropped on the way,' as the old woman had said. He was in the uniform of an officer's servant. McClintock and his men continued along the south coast of King William Island. On the summit of Cape Herschel they found the remains of an old, but empty, cairn. A smaller cairn was located containing a note from Hobson, one of McClintock's other searchers, who stated that they had found 'the record so ardently sought for of the Franklin expedition at Point Victory on the north west coast of King William Island, McClintock wrote:

The record is indeed a sad and touching relic of our lost friends, and to simplify its contents I will point out separately the double story it so briefly tells.

In the first place the record paper was one of the printed forms usually supplied to discovery ships for the purpose of being enclosed in bottles and thrown overboard at sea in order to ascertain the strength of the currents, and the person finding it is requested to send it to the Admiralty. It is in six different languages.

Upon it is written, apparently by Lieut. Gore, as follows: '28 of May, 1847. HM Ships Erebus and Terror wintered in the ice in lat. 70.05 N., long. 98.23 W … Having wintered in 1846-47 at Beechy Island in lat. 74.43.28 N.; long.

91.39.15 W., after having ascended Wellington Channel lat. 77 and returned by the west side of Cornwalis Island. Sir John Franklin commanding the expedition. All well. Party consisting of 2 officers and 6 men left the ships on Monday, 24th May, 1847.'

McClintock points out an error as to the Beechey Island entry, being 1846-47 instead of 1845-46.

McClintock's comments that seldom had an Arctic explorer met with such success as had Franklin's party up to this point. 'But alas,' he writes:

Round the margin of the paper upon which Lieut. Gore in 1847 wrote those words of hope and promise another hand had subsequently written the following words: 'April 25, 1848 – HM ships Erebus and terror were deserted on 22nd April 5 leagues N.N.W. of this, having been beset since 12th September, 1846. The officers and crews consisting of 105 souls under the command of Captain F. R. M. Crozier landed here in lat. 69.37.42 N.; long. 98.41 W. Sir John Franklin died on 11 June 1847, and the total loss by deaths in the expedition has been to this date 9 officers and 15 men. Signed F. R. M. Crozier, Captain and Senior Officer, James FitzJames, Captain H.M.S. Erebus. Can start tomorrow, 26th for Black Fish River [presumably the Black or Great Fish River].'

The note had been written by FitzJames and there was some additional marginal information about the transfer of the document from four miles to the northward near Point Victory, where it had been originally deposited by the late Commander Gore, to its present location. The word 'late' indicates he must have also died within the twelve months.

That was the last written word of the ill-fated expedition. Banbridge-born Captain Crozier had tried to save the remaining 105 men from a terrible death by retreating to the Hudson Bay territories by way of the Black, or Great Fish River which Franklin himself had explored in his Coppermine river expedition in 1821. However, the retreat ultimately proved futile and the men, already in a weakened state after months of deprivation, all perished on the journey.

Lieutenant Hobson reported to McClintock that he had found quantities of clothing and other articles lying about the cairn as though Franklin's men, fighting for their lives, had abandoned everything they thought superfluous. Later they found a battered boat with tattered clothing around, but no more written records. The boat had been built to go up the Black River, being mounted on a sledge to haul it over the ice. More relics were found including pieces of plate. The direction of the sledge, near which were found two skeletons, suggested that these men were returning to the ships. They had evidently been unable to keep pace with the others and were going back. There is also speculation that the survivors resorted to eating the flesh of their dead comrades, so perhaps the statue of Crozier in Banbridge is not only a monument to a failed explorer but maybe even 'a cannibal!'

10

IVEAGH AND THE GRATE

This is a wonderful tale by Richard P. Mackallay an old storyteller from Derryvore in County Down. The story was recorded in 1888. It has a real sense of the past, the people and life in rural County Down 125 years ago.

It was a cold, stormy evening in December, the wind blew in loud, angry gusts, and the rain fell in heavy, chilling showers. The party assembled in the parlour of a well-known tavern in Gilford, County Down did not regard the storm outside. A good fire blazed cheerfully in the grate, the table was covered with glasses, and a large jug of whiskey punch steamed in the centre. The circle seated about the table consisted of small farmers, shrewd, intelligent, and active – and all were in comfortable circumstances. They were animated with that spirit of humour and conviviality so common to their happy, lively countrymen, and they met after the important business of the day, to spend a social evening.

The host himself occupied a seat amongst them. He was a fine old man, with bright sparkling eyes, and an expressive countenance, his hair was thin and silvery, and was swept back from a broad high forehead, which indicated great intellectual abilities. He was a patriot of the right stamp, a popular orator, and deeply versed in Irish history. He was an accomplished musician, and handled the painter's brush with effect and judgement. Seated on a chair near the fire, at the head of the table, was Dan Kernan, the presiding genius of the scene. He was a wit and humorist, a general favourite, and wherever he went he kept the social circle in roars of merriment with his quaint sallies and tales. While uttering his witticisms, he never smiled – even when his auditors were convulsed with laughter; he looked round with a roguish twinkle in his eye, and cast a leer on them inexpressibly comic.

Amongst the rest of the company present was an English buyer who had come over to purchase linens for the London market. Being anxious to see Irishmen at home in the social circle, as he himself expressed it, he had sought the acquaintance of the host, and was by him introduced to the company present. Being aware of this presence, they were anxious to show off Dan to the best advantage, and he certainly did not disappoint their expectations, for he was high spirited and facetious on the occasion.

Poor Dan, he prided himself on his skill in the cultivation of flax and, after successfully operating in his own country, he went to Munster to teach the Southerns how to raise lint on improved principles. Whether the soil obstinately clung to old customs, and sternly refused to accept Whig Political Economy, or that he did not meet with congenial spirits, we do not know, but he did not succeed.

'This is a cold night, Dan,' observed one of the company.

'Yes, replied Dan, 'but we do not feel it, we are all well fortified against the storm,' and he glanced at the table.

'There's what will keep out the cold,' he said, looking at the jug of punch, 'and save the necessity of calling in the doctor.'

'You don't care much for the doctors?' asked another of the company.

'No,' he replied, 'I like to keep a decent distance from them. A hearty laugh is worth all the medicine in their shops. Better to hear it ringing in your ears, than hear the hooves of a doctor's horse rattling on your driveway. It proclaims heavy bills, a lingering illness with but slender hopes of a speedy recovery.

'You did not take much doctor's stuff in your time?' inquired another of the company.

'Not I, in troth,' answered Dan, 'I prefer this stuff to any of their nostrum,' and so saying he drained his tumbler.

'What say you to a tankard of ale?' inquired the Englishman.

'Thanks for your kindness, but there is no good in it,' replied Dan. It may do very well in a hurry to slake your thirst, but it makes you dull and loggish. Commend me to a glass of good old corn whisky, without any water in it, except when made in punch. It courses through the whole frame, from the very toes to the brain, driving out all crude humours and rendering you jovial and lively.'

'We believe you, Dan,' echoed the company; 'we'll take another glass, and you'll tell us a story, to keep us in good humour.'

'Troth will I,' said Dan, 'and it shall not be a tale stolen from foreign cheap periodical literature, displaying flimsy characters in unnatural positions, uttering stale unmeaning sentiments, and ending with a bad moral. I shall lay the scene in our own district, the hero shall be one of ourselves, well known to you all, exhibiting genuine Irish humour, impulsive courage, rash thoughtless daring, and pure generosity. After I have told it, if you don't say it is a good one, I'll give you leave to say the landlord here knows nothing about making punch, and I will match him at mixing a jug against any man from here to Dublin.'

'More power, Dan we are sure your story will be a good one. Take a glass to clear your throat and begin.'

'We wait, boys, till I light the pipe, and you'll see how I'll handle my subject.'

He lit his pipe, blew a huge cloud of smoke from his mouth, and commenced:

My friends, I am going to tell a story – not a tale of fiction, mind ye, but a pure matter-of-fact narrative – abounding with romantic incidents, combined with the grotesque and ludicrous, which, under the hand of a skilful writer, could be formed into a drama highly interesting and effective. As this enlightened English gentleman is present, I must depart from my usual familiar style, and couch my talk in more elegant phraseology.

The scene of our story is Banbridge – a town with which most people in the North of Ireland are familiar, as it is justly celebrated for having one of the best horse fairs in the kingdom, to which dealers from all parts of the Empire, and even foreigners, go to purchase a good breed of cattle. To you who know the town and its vicinity so well, it would be superfluous to give a description, but it might be interesting to this enlightened Englishman – who, I hope, will be induced to visit Banbridge often, and admire the scenery around it, and cultivate the acquaintance of as spirited and enlightened a community as in Christendom.

Banbridge is situated on a gentle eminence, in the centre of a highly-cultivated district, beautifully diversified with groves, and dotted over here and there with gentlemen's seats, like diamonds on the dress of a fair belle. The River Bann, like a silvery serpent, winds through the town, and in its northern course towards Lough Neagh, waters the beautiful and verdant valleys. That part of the valley of the Bann commencing above Banbridge, and extending beyond Gilford, to the celebrated vale of Moyallen, is perhaps the richest valley in all Ireland. Spinning and bleach mills, and weaving factories, are built at short distances from each other along the banks of the river, while the verdant turf around is covered with linen in the process of bleaching. The proprietors of these industrial establishments are distinguished by cultivated taste, great enlightenment, and genuine liberality, and they are animated by a sincere regard for the welfare of those in their employment. The working classes are distinguished by sober, steady conduct, and are as orderly a people as any in the Empire. It has been remarked that the waters of the Bann have a peculiar softness beyond that of any other river in the world, and impart a dazzling whiteness to the linen, which cannot be equalled in any other place, and justly gives the pre-eminence to this branch of Irish manufacture. In fact, a laundress in this happy region has only to take her clothes and a piece of soap to the waters of the Bann, and there, without the assistance of hot water, soda ash, or Harper Twelvetees' Celebrated Washing Powder, she can give a beautiful colour to her clothes, which would be sought for in vain in a patent washing establishment.

We must now return to Banbridge, the scene of our story. The principal street of this town is, or rather, I should say, was, as handsome a street as could be seen in any provincial town in the kingdom, until the gentlemen who had the management of the local affairs of the town, with a taste truly vandalic, took it into their heads to make a cutting up the centre of this beautiful street, for no apparent useful purpose, heaven knows, except to spoil the beautiful prospect from the centre of the town. The cutting has a most uncouth appearance, bearing a strong resemblance to a broad dry ditch, or an old gravel pit. This cutting or excavation, or whatever it may be called, has one useful, though it may be called a questionable purpose: it serves at night as a capital rendezvous for the idle and disorderly portion of the denizens, who can place 'hide-and-seek' with the police, and avoid the acquaintance these worthy functionaries would wish to make with them. The cutting about the centre is spanned by an unsightly bridge, which it would be hard to refer to any order of architecture, and therefore defies description. This excavation was the first public work executed by an Irishman, who afterwards rose to the highest eminence. This was the celebrated William Dargan, who acquired a European celebrity. He exhibited in his own person what Irish genius and perseverance can effect, against opposing difficulties, so great was his merit that his sovereign personally waited on him at his own residence, and offered him a title – an honour never before conferred on any Irishman. He had the greatness of soul to refuse this flattering mark of distinction, and while thanking the Queen for the proposed honour, he respectfully told her he was 'plain William Dargan – one of the people – and as such he should die'.

It is now time to introduce Iveagh, the hero of our tale, to you. He was reared in the vicinity of Banbridge, where he still survives, and gained great local celebrity by his eccentricities. He is a man considerably above six feet in height, and affords a fine specimen of the stalwart peasant; his shoulders are broad, his arms long, with sinews of iron, and his strength truly Herculean; his courage is impetuous, and of the reckless, daring kind which fears no odds, however great; he is distinguished by generosity and kindness of heart; he spends his money freely with a friend and while ready to raise his brawny hand to knock down an antagonist, he opens it as readily to dispense his last shilling to those who may require pecuniary assistance, for his is sensibly alive to the voice of distress. He loves Ireland with the fervour of a patriot, and is devotedly attached to her interests. In this part of the country, where unfortunately, party feeling divides the people, and causes many serious contests, he has been engaged in numerous conflicts, and though often facing fearful odds, he invariable came off conqueror.

At the time that this uncouth cutting in Banbridge, to which I have alluded, was in course of formation, our hero was then in his prime, and reigned in the pugilistic circle without a rival. Mr Dargan brought a number of navvies to execute the work, and among them was a tall, young, athletic, and active southern man, who had gained great fame as a bruiser, and had reigned the cock of the walk in his own country. It was soon whispered that here was a match for our hero and it was hinted to Iveagh that he might need to look sharp for it would take all his strength and courage to maintain his superiority in the pugilistic arena, or the new comer would strip him of his 'belts'. Iveagh, confident in this own prowess, laughed contemptuously at their insinuations. But chance brought him into collision with the navvy, in an odd kind of way.

Being in the summer fair of Banbridge, Iveagh had taken as much of the 'native' as put him in the right humour for

fun and frolic. He strolled down in the afternoon to the
end of the cut, and stood a while in conversation with
some friends, when two men, rather the worse of liquor,
began a fight beside him. Iveagh viewed the combat with
indifference, until a third man came forward and struck
at one of the combatants. Iveagh, who detested foul play,
seized the man by the collar and, flinging him down,
told him to lie there till the fight was over, or he would
break every bone in his skin. At this juncture a tall navvy
stepped forward.

'I say neighbour,' said he, addressing Iveagh, 'you handled
that fellow nicely.'

'Well, what's that to you,' replied Iveagh, gruffly, casting
an angry glance on the impudent intruder.

'Oh, nothing,' said the navvy, 'only you would not use
me so easily that way.'

'Every whit as easy, so take care of yourself,' said Iveagh.

'I rather doubt it, my fine fellow,' retorted the navvy,
surveying him with a swaggering stare.

'What are you looking at, you spalpeen?' said Iveagh
angrily, whose knuckles were now itching for the encounter.

'At you,' quietly retorted the navvy, 'it is an offence? A cat
may look on a king, and I have looked on as good men as
you in my time.'

'I'll close your pepper,' said Iveagh, 'if you look at me in
that way again,' and he raised his huge fist menacingly.

'Troth and if you do, you will be well paid, you long
looby,' retorted the navvy, and he folded his arms with an
insulting gesture.

'Take that you vagabond to learn you manners,' cried
Iveagh, and he struck him a blow almost weighty enough
to fell an ox.

The navvy returned the blow, and the two heroes engaged in a terrible combat; the conflict was maintained for some time, with skill, and undaunted bravery on each side; they seemed so equally matched, that it was hard to say which would eventually be the victor. The idlers, and loungers, rushed forward and formed a ring, loudly cheering the combatants, who continued the fight with undiminished fury. The police, hearing the noise, hurried to the melee. With fixed bayonets they pushed the people aside, and seizing Iveagh and his antagonist, bore them off as captives.

The 'black-hole,' which had formerly been in the old Market-House, was by then pulled down, and a temporary lock-up had been engaged at the farther end of another street; to this place Iveagh and his comrade were brought, they were conveyed to a room upstairs, and fastened to a grate by a chain passing round the leg of each, and locked to a bar of the grate. The police, after bidding them make the most of their comfortable quarters, laughed derisively and went out, locking the door behind them. Iveagh and his comrade were locked to the grate with their backs to the fireplace, in a position which prevented them from sitting down or standing upright. They remained silent for some time with rueful countenance, surveying their woeful condition. At length the navvy broke the silence.

'Iveagh,' said he, 'we are in a sorry plight, like two rats in a trap, and we cannot even light the pipe to have a whiff to comfort us. Bad luck to the peelers, anyhow, may they never have decenter work than hanging goats, or driving pigs, the blackguards. I hope I'll get revenge of them yet.'

'We are badly fixed, sure enough,' said Iveagh, 'but we must see if we can mend our state.'

Iveagh prided himself on his neatly formed ankle and small foot, and they were of great service to him just then, for, by a slight effort, he twisted his foot from his boot, and was freed from the chain in a moment.

'I am at liberty now,' said he, as he pulled on his boot, and walking towards the window, 'I'll soon be out of this.'

'Ah, Iveagh!' cried the navvy, 'surely you would not leave a fellow-sufferer in bondage.'

'Well, I would not like to do a dirty thing,' replied Iveagh, turning back. 'Let me have a look at your foot. Ah, bad cess to your hoof, you lark-heeled dog, your own pickaxe might as well be in the chain! You ought to be a good singer, for you are akin to the lark; and you might chant up here a gaol bird's song delightfully – I would myself sing you a verse of a prison melody, but we might alarm the peelers.'

'Ah, Iveagh don't be joking,' responded the navvy, 'but think of something to release me.'

'By dad it is no joking,' cried Iveagh, 'I can't see how I can free you, for your foot is as fast as the head of a cripple's crutch. Wait! Help me to pull out the grate, and maybe we can lessen a bar.

By their joint efforts they pulled the grate into the middle of the floor.

'That is so much done,' said Iveagh, with a knowing smile.

'But I don't see what good it has done,' responded the navvy, querulously.

'Whist you fool,' said Iveagh, 'never look at half-done work; but I must now have a look at the outside.

He raised the window and cautiously looked out; a large horse dunghill came up close to the wall behind. Iveagh leaped down. Several empty coops and hampers lay about the yard, these he collected together and formed a temporary stage which reached up to the window. On this he mounted.

'Now my boy,' said Iveagh, 'put out the grate and your leg with it, and get on my back.'

The navvy did so, and Iveagh was instantly running from the yard, and made across the country in the direction of a smith's shop, about a mile off Banbridge.

Here let us pause a moment, to take a glance at Iveagh and his comrade as they moved along. There was the colossal figure of Iveagh with the navvy, almost as tall as himself, mounted on his back, to which he clung as firmly as did the old man of the sea to the back of the veracious sailor, Sinbad. The leg to which the grate was suspended was flung over the shoulder of Iveagh, who cleared the ditches with the agility of the greyhound. It was a sight indeed, to which alone the unmatchable pencil of a Maclise or Cruikshank could do justice.

Iveagh and his comrade soon reached the smith's shop. When they entered the shop, the smith was absent in Banbridge, but his wife, surprised at their appearance, came forward as they entered.

'Gracious goodness,' she exclaimed, 'Iveagh, is it you? Who, or what is this you have brought with you, and how came the man to be locked to the grate?'

'Whist, woman,' replied Iveagh, 'listen, he was a State prisoner, confined in Kilmainham, for helping O'Connell to Repale; he was locked to the grate, and forced to turn the spit for the governor's dinner every day, and was nearly roasted to death. He made his escape, and travelled down by night, carrying the grate with him, and I met with him in the fields a while ago.'

'Ah, the villains!' exclaimed the credulous, but compassionate woman, 'to treat a Christian man so barbarously. I must make him a rousing cup of tea, for I am sure he is nearly starved.'

'Do,' said Iveagh, 'he needs it; but where's your husband. I want a cowld chisel.'

'My husband is in Banbridge, but will soon be home. The tools are there; you can get them for yourself.'

Iveagh got the cold chisel, and soon freed the navvy from the grate. When the navvy found himself at liberty he extended his hand to Iveagh.

'Ten thousand thanks for your kindness,' he said. 'I shall never forget it, and we'll never fight again.'

'Not to the next time,' said Iveagh, 'but I'm glad you're free anyhow.'

'I have an old shilling,' said the navvy, 'that never seen the light. We could get the worth of it of whisky.'

'I have another,' said Iveagh, 'and we'll soon have a drop. Where is the little fellow,' he said, glancing around the shop for the smith's son. 'Here my brave boy,' he said addressing the lad, 'run away to Banbridge for the worth of this of whisky. Look for your father and tell him to come home; but mind, don't mention anything about this man or I, and here are some coppers to buy yourself gingerbread.'

Iveagh and his comrade went into the kitchen. The smith and the little messenger soon returned and the party sat down round the social hearth, and made a night of it. Iveagh laughed heartily at having tricked the police, and about daylight they parted with mutual expressions of goodwill.

Some days later the police summoned Iveagh and his comrade for stealing the grate, and they also summoned the smith for receiving stolen goods. On the day of the expected trial the little Court House was densely crowded, it having been generally known that Iveagh was to appear on a summons to answer a charge of a novel kind. There were three Magistrates on the bench. The chairman was a highly intelligent gentleman and well known in the mercantile world, having been extensively engaged in the linen trade. He was thoroughly acquainted with the peculiar humour of his countrymen, and he found that leniency did more than severity to keep the county tranquil. The other two Solons were of that stolid, saturnine cast, who do not feel risibility in themselves, and could not tolerate gaiety in others. To laugh they considered a grave sin, and to perpetrate a practical joke, they considered a mortal offence, which ought to be met with severed condign punishment. These two functionaries regarded the offence committed by Iveagh and his companion as of the most serious kind, which ought to be severely dealt with.

When the charge against Iveagh and his comrade was recited, and they were asked what they had to say to it, Iveagh drew himself up to this full height and looked round the courts with the air of an honest man, charged with an offence from which he shrinks with indignation.

'What, me charged with robbery?' he exclaimed, 'by gor that's quare, no one who knows me will for a moment credit it. It's true I'm a rash, thoughtless fellow, ready to drink and fight, but I drink my own, and I scorn to do a mean or dishonest action.'

'So do I,' cried the navvy indignantly, 'I have travelled over the three kingdoms, and worked in many a place, and never took the value of a pin from any one. I can earn a shilling and spend it, but I do nothing dishonest, I was better taught, for tho' I wear the navvy's jacket, I am not the ignorant clown you would suppose. I admit the charge of carrying off the grate, but it was to get myself freed from it. The police had no right to lock me and my companion to it, like two turnspit dogs, as we committed no felony, and only engaged in a bit of a shindy, without any malice on either side.'

The smith stood there, his face begrimed with coal dust, and his apron tucked aside in his belt. 'Well, by gad,' said he, 'this is an odd charge entirely. Me charged with receiving stolen goods; that beats anything I ever heard. I buy my own stuff and work it honestly for my customers. Somebody brought an ugly old grate to my shop when I was out, but I did not know where it came from, and it lies there for whoever it belongs to.'

The two junior magistrates were for treating Iveagh and his comrade severely, regarding it as a very great offence for them to set authority at defiance by breaking out of prison.

The chairman dissented, he considered it should be regarded as a very trivial offence, he observed that the police were partly to blame, to place two honest men who had only engaged in a drunken squabble in so humiliating a position. It was natural, he said, when they found themselves so slightly guarded, that they should attempt to free themselves from their strange situation, and no other resource offered out to carry the grate to free themselves from it. He said they should pay some regard to the heroic conduct of Iveagh, who, forgetting all enmity hazarded his own safety to free his antagonist from his bonds. It was plain, he observed, the smith knew nothing of the bringing of the grate to his shop and therefore the charge against him must be dismissed, and the ends of justice would be fully answered, by inflicting small fines on Iveagh and his companion.

After some discussion the bench finally agreed to this decision, and Iveagh and his comrade turned to leave the court.

As Iveagh was passing by the disappointed police, he addressed them with a knowing leer, 'I say boys, the next goat you hunt down, send me word, and I'll bring you the grate to tether her to; it will make a fine crib to feed her out of. You may have new milk for your tea, and you can save your odd coppers to buy a glass of ale when you are dry.'

With this display of defiance he left the court amidst the cheers of the people, which the magistrate in vain attempted to check.

11

HADDOCK'S GHOST

This story was recorded in some old Banbridge annals in 1886 by an anonymous writer and is a great ghost story, worthy of any collection of ghostly tales. The story itself takes place during the mid-1600s in Dromore, County Down, and is an interesting one for different reasons. The first is that it was supposedly investigated by Bishop Jeremy Taylor, who, according to his secretary's report, 'Was satisfied the apparition was true and real'. The next is that a full account of it (which is still preserved) was written by the bishop's secretary to Dr Henry More, a learned English academic, who inserted it in his edition of Glamil's work on witchcraft. And finally, the case was thought worthy of a citation by no less eminent person than Mr Richard Baxter in his book Certainty of the World of Spirits. *So let us begin …*

In 1657 James Haddock, who had lived in Malone, near Belfast where he held a farm under Lord Donegall, died, leaving behind a widow and an only son. Shortly before his death he had arranged with Lord Donegall's agent for a renewal of his lease on the farm, and he also arranged that the name of his son should be inserted into the contract. For this promised renewal a stipulated sum was agreed but although Haddock had paid this in part, he died before the whole amount was covered and consequently the new lease was made but never sealed.

Not long after Haddock's death, his widow married another man called Davis, to whom she bore a son. On the birth of his son Davis put his name, instead of the name of the rightful heir, Haddock's own son, into the new lease on which he paid the remainder of the settlement that Haddock had left owing. This event took place five years after Haddock's death and it was around this time that strange things started to happen.

The first of these incidents occurred when a man called Francis Taverner, who was a servant of Lord Donegall, was riding home one night from Hillsborough in County Down. He was confronted near Drumbridge by a spectral-apparition, which claimed to be James Haddock and insisted he be listened to. He told Taverner he had business to deliver to him but Taverner, terrified by the ghostly apparition, declined to listen and galloped off as fast as he could. But the spirit did not give up easily. He re-appeared to Taverner the following night and this time declared his business. The spectral Haddock told Taverner to go and speak to his widow, now Mrs Davis, on his behalf and tell her not to allow the name of her second son to be substituted on the lease of the farm for the name of her firstborn. But Taverner would not be swayed; he refused to relate the message to the widow. The ghost, however, was relentless and haunted the poor servant without any respite. Taverner was so tormented that he went to Belfast to stay with a friend, hoping to escape the ghost's visits. But even there the apparition followed him. One night the ghost appeared to him in a fit of terrible rage, eyes burning like hot coals and its mouth stretched wide open in a hideous maw. The phantom threatened to tear Taverner to pieces if he did not relate the message. Terrified, Taverner went the following morning to his master's house, Lord Donegall, and told him of the strange and frightening events. Donegall's chaplain, Revd James South, was there and strongly advised that Taverner go to the widow and deliver the message. He even offered to go along with Taverner to Malone and speak to the widow. Taverner accepted the offer and on their way they called into see Dr Lewis Downes, then minister of Belfast, who on hearing the matter warned them that they had to be sure that this errand was not dictated by an evil spirit. Taverner remembered Haddock in his life and said he was a good man with high moral standards, so the spirit was sure to have good intentions for his widow.

Eventually all three men went to see Mrs Davis but she declined to comply with her late husband's request, saying that she would not act on the orders from a ghost.

Poor old Taverner was visited by the spirit again that night and had to pass on the bad news; needless to say he was terrified. The ghost then ordered him to go directly to the people who executed Haddock's last will and testament. This is exactly what Taverner did. One of these people was Bishop Jeremy Taylor. When he heard the story he requested a private meeting with Taverner at his ecclesiastical court in Dromore. There Taverner was examined by the bishop on this 'strange scene of providence', as he referred to it as. After listening to Taverner's tale the bishop was convinced that the apparition was 'true and real'. Before dismissing

Taverner, Bishop Taylor advised him, the next time the spirit appeared, to ask it these following questions: 'Whence are you?, Are you a good or a bad spirit?, Where is your abode?, What station do you hold?, How are you regimented in the other world?, And what is the reason that you are allowed to appear for the relief of your son in so small a matter, when so many widows and orphans are oppressed in the world, and none of their relations appear from thence to right them as you do?'.

On the very night that Taverner received this list of questions from the bishop, the spirit again appeared to him. He told the ghost that he had been to see the executors of his will, as he had desired, but nothing came of it. Taverner then proceeded to put to the spirit the questions with which he had been furnished by the bishop. In reaction to this the ghost became solemn and contemplative and then he spoke these words, 'I wish you no harm Francis Taverner, but I cannot be at rest. Where I have come from, the only peace I will find there is to make amends here, in this world I have now departed from. I swore an oath to my only son that he should inherit what I had, without his name on the lease he is entitled to nothing. I vowed upon my life that my son should have this. My life may be at an end but my word still holds strong'. He then insisted that there must be a trial with the executors to set things straight. Taverner exclaimed there was no point as there were no witnesses. The ghost replied, 'I will be present, and I will appear when called upon'. With that, the ghost vanished into thin air.

The case was brought forward at to a trial in Carrickfergus. During the course of the trial the counsel for the executors of Haddock's will ridiculed Taverner's story about his interview with Haddock's disembodied spirit as being incredible and

absurd. But Taverner stood by his story and the counsel taunted and mocked him to bring forth and call for his spectral witness. And that is exactly what he did; he called three times for Haddock to appear. After the third calling a clap of thunder shook the courthouse to its very foundations, terrifying the congregation. A figure appeared at the witness table and a voice was heard asking, 'Is that enough?' There was Haddock, standing there with an ethereal mist surrounding his body. The terrified jury at once brought the verdict against the executors and in favour of Haddock's son.

Shortly afterwards the spirit appeared for the last time to Taverner. It thanked him for his services and loyalty and then reached out and touched him. A shiver went through Taverner's body but now he felt no fear and in fact he felt that some form of blessing had been bestowed upon him.

Taverner was never visited by the ghost again but always felt a protective presence about him. Whenever opportunity arose he would visit the Davis household and make sure that all was well and offer his help wherever possible.

12

BILLY AND THE CHANGELING OF GLASCAR

Come away, O human child!
To the waters and the wild
With a faery, hand in hand.
For the world's more full of weeping,
Than you can understand.

(From 'The Stolen Child' by William Butler Yeats, 1889)

This beautiful and heart-warming tale was first recorded by the Revd J.B. Lusk of Glascar, County Down in 1925. I had the privilege to find it deep in the archives of County Down's rich folk history and I have taken it upon myself to reiterate this story for this collection of folk tales.

Over 200 years ago the desire for news, gossip and stories was as strong as it is today, but for the majority of the people living in and around Glascar in County Down, there were neither newspapers nor novels available, and even if they did obtain such items the ability to read evaded most of the population. So how did they gain new knowledge of the world around them? It is hard to imagine in today's 'Information Age', with access to the world wide web and mobile phones, how people went about transferring information long distances, particularly as many of them could not read or write, making letters of little use. Instead reports, news and stories were spread by the beggars who travelled the country roads. Beggars were a common sight, even before the famine, as ordinary folk were dependent for their food supply from their own harvests; in bad seasons many were driven by the fear of starvation to beg for a living. Few who took to the roads returned to the humdrum ways of hard, loveless labour. What they at first looked on as a curse they came to regard it as a blessing in disguise. At every home, with very few exceptions, beggars received a handful of oatmeal or a few spuds. They carried only their beds with them, consisting of a pair of blankets and a quilt.

These beggars were made welcome to a night's lodging in any of the more modest, less affluent homes. They paid for their accommodation by the news they related, news they had gathered on their wide travels, songs and ballads they collected and of course wondrous stories. Indeed their arrival was looked forward to by young and old. Some of the beggars saw themselves as entertainers, some even as celebrities and felt that houses had been honoured by their company.

According to Lusk, by the end of the eighteenth century the recognised chief celebrity of this ragged fraternity was Billy the Beggarman. Billy occasionally visited the Glasgar neighbourhood and Lusk states that his visits were like a royal progress, in which he received the homage of his subjects and the offerings of his admirers. His sophistication and elegance were the wonder and envy of many and, like in today's pop culture where young people try to emulate their favourite rock star or actor, the younger generation at the time wished to imitate him.

According to this illustrious vagabond, there were few countries in the world where he had not fought and fewer still that he not visited. When asked how foreigners spoke, which was always a great subject of curiosity, he would reply 'Some make a kind of rumblin' noise and others make a sound like cats spittin''. And not to mention the wild beasts, strange creatures and terrible monsters he encountered and he had scars to prove it. He had a grand, majestic manner about him, like some hobo monarch, but was described as being a big, affable, kindly, jolly, hairy-faced man with a powerful voice and grand company to be around.

Unlike his peers, he visited only the more respectable houses, but on the rare occasion where lady luck was not smiling on him, he went to men of low estate. His method of breaking new ground was to stop some yards from the door of the abode and chant this piece of his own composition:

Pity kind gentle folk, friends of humanity;
Cold blows the wind and the night's coming on;
Spare me some food for my mother and charity;
Spare me some food and bid me be gone.

The reference to his mother is either for the sake of rhyme or some class of poetic license as he always travelled alone.

Lusk speaks of a very old man named Jimmie he knew when he was a young man, shortly after he came to Glascar, who claimed to have heard some of Billy's stories during his boyhood. One might think that the story was told to rattle a young and innocent minister arriving in a new parish, but

Lusk sates the old man showed all the signs and signals that he believed every word of it. And the old man told the story with such conviction and zeal that the tale had stayed with Lusk all his days. And this is the story that Lusk was told about Billy the Beggarman and The Changeling of Glascar:

Early one cold and windy morning in December, one of the local lads of Glascar was startled to see Billy the Beggarman running towards him out of the woods, like a man possessed.

'Oh Jimmie,' cried Billy, 'I got the most desperatest scare I ever got in me life and if ye listen I'll tell you, but you must never tell it to another man or mortal'. Billy had been on his rounds over in the Ballynafern side and had called to a house with 'dacent folk'. They gave him two good handfuls of meal and wee bit of bacon. As he was leaving the master gave him a kind of half wink and told him, he could get him something that would warm his heart on this cold night. He knew a man not far from there who was making a drop of the rare auld mountain dew 'Poteen' and would give Billy a dram on his account.

The man brought Billy to a wee sod house. Inside was a man working a still. The brewer gave Billy a mug full of the stuff and said, 'No clash o' this in the country, and what's more you need never show your nose in this side again or you'll get me in trouble'.

'Oh! You can trust Billy,' replied the man who brought him in.

Well they had a great time taking a sup of the good stuff and before Billy knew, it was coming up on eleven o'clock. Although the company was good and the drink was flowing, Billy had the sense to make his excuses to leave.

He decided to take the higher ground and come around by the west, as there had been a lot of rain and the river down in the Glen would have be difficult and dangerous to cross in the dark.

When he got up to Ballynaskeag Hill it was a grand night. There was a touch of frost and Billy knew this by, 'The throbbin' and the leppin' o' the stars, and the mist that lay like dark loughs, in the hollows'.

Billy was in no hurry; the sights and sounds were wondrous all around him. As Billy explained himself, 'I was feelin' comfortable and content, indeed sometimes the stars was whirlin' round me, and I sat down once or twice to look at them'. But with all Billy's star gazing he missed his turning for Glascar and it wasn't long before he found himself lost.

After a time he came to a big hedge and he figured that his right road was on the other side of it. He decided that his best course of action would be to jump over the hedge, rather than lose himself further by following it to its end and going around it. So he proceeded to climb the hedge, which was not an easy task in the dark and under the influence of strong alcohol. When he got to the top he grabbed a branch to steady himself. As he lowered himself over the other side the branch gave way and Billy landed heavily on his back, hitting his head on something hard. The last thing he remembered was rolling down into a deep hollow and then everything went black.

How long he lay there for he couldn't tell, but when he came to he could not move either his hand or his foot, it was as though he was tied down all over with threads. It also appeared that he must have grown miles and miles in length for it seemed to him that his head was resting up against Glascar Hill like a pillow with his feet were laying a few miles away down in Loughbrickland. After a while he felt that he was swelling up, rising upwards towards the stars as though he would eventually fill the whole world.

Whilst he was lying there pondering about all of this, the most beautiful music he had ever heard started playing all around him. It sounded like flutes and fiddles with birds singing in-between. 'Oh! It would have wiled the heart out of ye,' said Billy to Jimmie. 'I opened my eyes, and there was a light all about me like a lot o' candles seen through thin paper. I saw then where I was and my heart stood still for a minute, and then it raced like a gallopin' horse. I was that scared I must have fainted for a bit. Well Jimmie there I was on top of Derrydrummuck fort, and I swear on my soul, the fairies were out at their diversions. If I had been outside the ring all the chains in Ireland wouldn't have held me'.

Billy explained to Jimmie that if you are outside a fairy ring when you hear the music, you're safe enough, but if you're inside they can do what they like with you. So there he was inside the ring and there was nothing he could do except lie there and look on.

After a while the fear left Billy and he figured that they would not hurt him, shur what would they want with a poor old beggar-man who never harmed anybody? He lay there gazing around and saw a hole in the far side of the ring that he hadn't noticed before. As he looked at it, out trooped a whole host of wee men and lasses. They came out just like bees out of a hive. The men were about two feet tall, and they had on cocked hats of all colours and green or dark-coloured coats with long tails and pockets and long waistcoats with gold buttons. They had white knee-breeches and blue stockings and shoes with silver buckles. The lasses were hardly as big as the men; they had beautiful shoes that

shone like gold and wide skirts that came down to near their
ankles and bodices that were laced across with all kinds of
narrow coloured ribbons. Around their shoulders they had
wee shawls of net-work that glistened as if they had been
laid out in the frost. Their hair was piled up on top of their
heads, and sparkled as though a lot of wee stars had got
mixed up in it.

   Last of all came a big girl that looked younger than any
of them; she looked like she was about five or six years old,
but she was of enormous size. She was dressed like the rest,
but she had a long rod in her hand with a light at the top of
it that shone one minute green then yellow then blue and
then red. She gave it a wave and they all made a ring around
her and began to dance. It was a breathtaking sight, all the
'wee crathurs' circling round her, keeping time to the music
and dancing as light as feathers. As they danced they sang a
song that went like this:

> By the sheen of the stars
> By the light of the moon
> Under these our rights are done.
>
> The still night and muffled streams
> Gleaming frost and whitened earth
> O! These are for our mirth.
>
> Hence! Ye earth-born mortals, hence!
> Come not near our wonted haunts
> Taint ye not our ancient homes!

Then Billy saw one of them lifting up his hand suddenly,
and they all stopped. In a powerful voice for such a small

creature he shouted, 'Our gentle thorn is injured. Look! And see what has performed this heinous act'.

They rushed over by where Billy was lying. The fear came back on him like a wave and he began to gasp as if he were drowning. As they gathered around him they let out such a terrible screech that turned Billy's blood to ice.

Billy knew well enough not to open his mouth until he was spoken to, for if you speak to the fairies before they speak to you, you'll never speak again. The one who stopped the dance stepped up to him and said, 'Rash mortal, why do you dare disturb us?'

Billy replied by trying to explain how he had got lost and meant them no harm or disturbance.

With that one of the fairies rushed towards them crying 'O King! It is he who has broken our gentle thorn'.

The wee man, whom Billy had just learnt was their king, looked at him severely, then raised his hand and shouted, 'Punish him!' With that, the rest of them pointed their fingers at Billy and wherever they pointed an agonizing pain surged though his body. Every bone in his body felt like it was being wrenched out of its socket. This seemed to last for an awful long time, he thought he could take no more, as he said to Jimmie, 'I gave a groan thinkin' I was departin''. But just when Billy was about to give up hope of survival the big lass came up near him and cried out, 'O King, I must speak to him!'.

'No, no', replied the King.

'Oh I must', the girl implored.

The King relented and told the girl she could have a wee while, but mustn't be long. With that they all scudded back into the hole and she sat down on the grass beside him. She put out her hand and touched him, instantly all pain left his body. He looked up at her with gratitude, it was then that he saw she was just a child, but spoke as well and sophisticated as an educated adult woman in a child's voice.

The child asked him what had brought him there and he explained that he had got lost and did not realise he was so close to the fort, let alone a fairy ring.

'Did you come here to spy on the fairies?' asked the child. 'Tell the truth, it will serve you best.' Billy swore on the 'Bible' and the 'Question Book' that he was no spy. When he mentioned the 'Question Book' he saw that the child believed him. She asked Billy if he had any children and he told her he had none, 'what would a poor beggar-man be doing with children?', he asked.

The girl seemed saddened by this and said it was a pity as she would have liked to talk about the children.

She told Billy that he should not have come to this place, but she was glad that he did. 'Who are you child?' asked Billy bewildered.

'I am a "changeling",' explained the child. 'You see, when I was a wee baby the fairies saw that I was going to be badly treated all my life and have awful hard time, so they stole me from my mother and father and left some wicked creature in my place that caused them awful bother and then left when there was nothing left to take. I can see you're wondering how I know, and think I couldn't remember such a thing. Babies that stay with humans forget as they grow older, but babies that come to fairyland remember everything. I remember how they petted me and cared for me, though it's so very long ago. Babies that come here never grow bigger than I am now. I have had a beautiful time here.

I can go where I like and often play with children among you, though they don't see me and don't know that I am with them. I make everything go wrong for bad-tempered and peevish and cruel children. They fall and hurt their heads, bite their tongues and the really bad ones I frighten in their sleep. But the good-natured ones, who try to help others, I make contented and happy, and when they are asleep I bring them to fairyland and show them the beautiful things I have seen. I tell the fairies to help the grown-up people with their work who are generous and kind and to watch over their homes and protect them from all harm and evil spirits. But I plague the ungenerous, unthankful and unkind. I open the gaps and make their cattle stray, I make their watch-dogs sleep and I send rats and mice into their hay-stacks and houses. I have such powers to help and hinder the good and bad of this world, but I still sometimes miss to talk to those who know nothing about fairyland and tell them all about it, as I am talking to you now.'

The changeling explained to Billy that the fairies didn't like her talking to other humans in case she decided to leave them. But she said she would never leave, and wouldn't go back even if she could. 'What will they do with me?' asked the poor beggar-man as he heard the trooping fairies returning. 'They hate anyone who spies on them or anyone who digs about a fort, and they will always punish them. But they always keep a changeling like me who understands something about humans; for fear that they should become very harsh and cruel and punish mortals too severely. I will speak to the King on your behalf and you must do what I bid you, or something terrible will happen to you. If he says "be gone" make a mighty effort, though you may think that you are tied down, and jump to your feet and run for your life. Don't under any circumstances look behind you and never go near the fort again as long as you live.'

Well Billy took everything in and thanked the changeling profusely for her clemency. Within seconds the fairies were all about him. He could see the changeling speaking to the King, but he could not make out what was being said.

Suddenly the King stepped up towards him and shouted 'Be gone!'. With all his strength, and although it was agony, Billy leapt to his feet and took to his heels. He didn't care about the ditches and hedges but just tore over and through everything. They were after him like a swarm of bees, prodding him all over with tiny spears. In the corner of his eye Billy could see one wee ruffian driving a spear into his hip joint. He could have easily walloped him across the head but his fear and wisdom made him think it wiser to do nothing except run. He only stopped when he came across wee Jimmie, out of breath and out of his mind.

Well some years later Billy the Beggarman passed on and many of his stories went with him and are now lost. Some of the old-timers say that his ghost can be seen on a certain night of the year at the fort, sitting on a rock with a ring of little lights dotted around him, telling stories and singing songs and that there can be heard the sound of a wee child's laughter. But if you ever witness this do not get too close, make a wish, keep it to yourself and quietly go on about your business.

13

ALEXANDER SLOANE

Alexander Sloane had seven sons, of whom the eldest, James, was twice Member for Killyleagh in King William's Parliament. He is also listed as the tenant of 300 acres in the Ards, at a rental of £5, and again of a holding in Lisnaw at £22, and as the possessor of a house in Killyleagh Town, County Down. This is no doubt the house of which some remains are still to be seen in a side street in Killyleagh, with a stone tablet recording its building by Alexander Sloane. This house, which presented a by no means imposing appearance, was the birth-place (1660) of Hans, the youngest of the seven sons born to Alexander Sloane. Nothing more is heard of the rest of the Sloane family, but Hans seems to have risen with extraordinary rapidity. He was a delicate youth, and this probably accounts for his studious disposition. This may have been the reason why, instead of remaining at home or entering Trinity College, Dublin, he was sent abroad. We find him, while still in his teens, studying medicine at Paris and Montpellier, and graduating MD at the University of Orange at the age of twenty-three. Two years later he was a

fellow of the Royal Society, and shortly after he set out for
Jamaica as physician to the Duke of Albemarle, governor
of that colony. It was here that he began that wonderful
natural history collection that was the nucleus of the British
Museum. Returning to London in 1689, he settled in
practice in Bloomsbury Square, and quickly became one of
the greatest figures of his day.

Although he spent large sums on his collections of various
sorts, and was noted for his charities, Sloane amassed a
considerable fortune. In 1712 he purchased the Manor of
Chelsea from the Cheyne family and in 1716 he was made
a baronet. He founded the famous Physic Garden, which
he presented to the Society of Apothecaries on condition
that 'it should at all times be continued as a physic garden
as a manifestation of the power, and wisdom and goodness
of God in creation, and that the apprentices might learn
to distinguish good and useful plants from hurtful ones'.
The garden, with its cedars and other rare trees, is still one
of the ornaments of the Chelsea Embankment, and in the
middle stands a statue by Rysbrack of the generous donor. It
is not recorded that Sloane ever returned to Ireland, or that
Killyleagh benefited by his extensive charities, but his name
was evidently identified with his native county, for when
Walter Harris wrote his *Ancient and present State of the County
of Down* in 1744 he dedicated it to Sloane, and dedications at
that time generally implied financial assistance.

Sloane's taste for collecting seems to have made him the
butt of the satirists of the day, to whom scientific research
was a harmless mania. Pope speaks of 'books for Meade and
butterflies for Sloane'; Young sneers at him as 'the foremost
toyman of his time'; and Hone, in his *Year Book*, refers to
the 'Nicknackatory'. Sloane, however, knew more than

his critics of the invaluable nature of his museum, and he decided that it should belong to the nation. But he decided also that the nation should show that it appreciated its good fortune by paying his executors £20,000 in return – a sum probably not one-fourth the value of the collection. His library consisted of upwards of 42,000 printed books alone, 'perhaps the fullest and most curious in the world with regard to the several branches of natural history and physic.' There were also 3,000 manuscripts and 69,352 articles, 'the most valuable private collection, perhaps public one,' says the enthusiastic Harris, 'that has ever yet appeared on earth.'

In spite of his early delicacy, Sloane lived till the ripe age of ninety-three. Born in the last days of the Commonwealth, he had the probably unique experience of living though six reigns – those of Charles II, James II, William III, Anne, George I, and George II. 'His mental vigour,' we are told, 'long outlived his powers of locomotion; to the last it was his delight to be wheeled in a chair about his museum and examine its contents. He appears to have acted on the maxim he often repeated to this patients, 'I never take physic when I am well; when I am ill I take little, and only such as has been well tried.' He died in 1753, and was buried in Chelsea Churchyard, where the appropriate and artistic monument, designed by Wilton, the sculptor and Royal Academician, attracts the notice of all visitors. His one son, Hans, died an infant, and so his property went to found the fortunes of a family that did not bear his name.

In the article on Sir Hans Sloane what his contemporaries called his 'nicknacktory' is referred to. Sir Charles Hanbury Williams was asked by him to send him all the curiosities he could find when travelling in foreign lands. In reply he sent the following poetical catalogue of rarities:

I've ravaged air, earth, seas, and caverns,
Mountains and hills, and towns and taverns,
And greater rarities can show
That Gresham's children ever knew.
From Carthage brought the sword I'll send,
Which brought Queen Dido to her end.

The stone whereby Goliath died,
Which cures the headache, well applied.
A whetstone, worm exceeding small,
Time used to whet his scythe withal.
The pigeon, stuff'd which Noah sent
To tell him when the water went.

A ring I've got of Samson's hair,
The same which Dalilah did wear.
St Dunstan's tongs, which storey shows
Did pinch the devil by the nose.
The very shaft, as all my see,
Which cupid shot at Anthony.

And, which above the rest I prize,
A glance of Cleopatra's eyes.
Some strains of eloquence which hung
In Roman times on tully's tongue.
I've got a ray of Phoebus' shine,
Found in the bottom of a mine.

A layer's conscience larger and fair,
Fit for a judge himself to werr.
In a thumb-vial you shall see,
Close corked, some drops of honesty,

Which, after searching kingdoms round,
At last were in a cottage found.

An antidote, if such there be,
Against the charms of flattery.
I ha'nt collected any care:
Of that there's plenty everywhere.
But, after wondrous labours spent,
I've got one grain of rich content.

This my wish, it is my glory,
To furnish your nicknacktory.

14

THE GHOST GIRL OF BALLYMULLAN

The death of a loved one is always a devastating experience. But nothing is as devastating the death of a child. And the circumstances in which the death took place may mean that the spirit and energy of the child lingers on in a most powerful manner. Researchers of supernatural activity state that many sightings of ghosts which appear as children are connected with a terrible event which took place with that particular child. There are many cases of 'child ghosts' throughout Ireland and indeed the world, and one of the most tragic tales is that which was told throughout County Down known as 'the girl of Ballymullan'.

Ballymullan is a small townland in County Down and although the area has always been peaceful and quiet, it was renowned as a haunted place during the 1920s and 1930s, due to unexplained entities which were seen on one of its roads.

In July of 1929 a tradesman was driving a horse and cart along this road when up ahead of him he saw a young girl standing at the side of the road. As he approached her, his horse became uneasy and anxious and when he passed he saw she was as white as a sheet, her face was gaunt, her eyes dark and hollow, and her mouth hung open like an entrance into the abyss. The girl was quite close to the cart as it was passing but she paid no attention to it whatsoever. This surprised the tradesman as children always asked him for a lift. After passing the girl he pulled over and jumped from the cart to see if she was alright.

But when he turned around to speak to her, the girl was nowhere to be seen. Thinking that she must have fallen down the embankment, he ran to see where she was. He was shocked to discover that there was no one there. The young girl had vanished. The poor man stood in total disbelief and didn't realise until it was too late and his horse had bolted. He had to run down the road after the horse, which was still running and whinnying with fear. Thankfully the animal eventually came to a standstill a short distance away. When he reached the horse it was so distressed that he decided to walk alongside it in order to calm it down.

Further along the road he noticed a small cottage and approached it to ask if he could have some water for the horse. He told the elderly couple who lived in the house what he had just experienced and was told, without any hesitation, that what he had just seen was the 'Ghost Girl of Ballymullan'.

The couple went on to tell the tradesman about other sightings of the girl over the years and the tragedy which the apparitions were associated with. They told of how a young girl had been tragically killed on that stretch of road when she fell from a lorry back in 1917. The old couple said that she had been from Belfast and that her brother and sister were with her at the time and they had seen her die.

After getting the water for his horse the tradesman thanked the couple for their hospitality and consideration and he continued on his journey.

The tradesman, who was a curious soul, enquired further about the girl and the accident, but there were no records for the year 1917 and nothing was revealed to confirm the story that he had heard. There was nothing to show that anyone from Belfast had been killed in that area at that time. On further investigation, however, it turned out that the story from the elderly couple was true, but they had been wrong about the year in which it took place. It was revealed that in June 1912 a young girl was killed at the area where the sightings occurred, she had been from Belfast, she did fall from a lorry and she had been with her brother and sister when it occurred.

The story goes that on 22 June 1912, a large number of children connected with the Cregagh Presbyterian Church in Belfast were taken on a day trip to Helen's Bay which was organised by the church minister, the Revd David Stewart. When the children arrived they were given their lunch at noon and afterwards they took part in a number of games and activities on the beach, with the winners receiving small toys as prizes for their efforts. There was a wonderful atmosphere and the air was filled with the sound of laughter and excitement. Afterwards the children were given refreshments of lemonade which had been delivered to Helen's Bay for them by the Co-Operative Society as a gesture of goodwill. The driver, Samuel Johnstone, who brought the drinks had to wait for all the empty bottles. Whilst he was waiting the children begged him for a ride on the lorry. Since he was doing nothing he agreed but stated that all the children could not go at once; instead,

he would make a few trips to Crawfordsburn. One of the children was twelve-year-old Florence Gibson, who could have gone on one of the first trips but wanted to wait and go with her brother and sister, Harry and Maggie. When their turn came all the children climbed aboard and settled down on to the back of the lorry. As it made its journey along the twisting road they were all laughing and cheering with exhilaration. But then the lorry came to a sharp turn and skidded and the jolt this caused made several of the children fall off. Florence Gibson fell head first onto the road and was killed instantly when her neck broke. Three other children named Robert Magee, aged fifteen, Lizzie Miller, aged eleven, and Lily Hamilton aged thirteen were all badly injured. It was a horrible scene: the air that was a moment before filled with cries of joy and excitement was now filled with cries of agony and terror, and the limp and lifeless body of little Florence Gibson lay shattered on the side of the road. The rest of the children were either hysterical or in shock. The unfortunate lorry driver was beside himself with remorse and attempted to assist the children, but there was so much confusion and panic that his efforts were futile.

After the terrible accident Dr Robert Bailey, deputy coroner for North Down, held an inquest on Monday 24 June 1912, at the Crawfordsburn Inn. It was indeed a sombre and macabre gathering as the body of the little girl was laid out on a table in the main meeting room of the inn. The first witness called was Thomas Gibson, brother of the deceased, who identified the remains.

Samuel Johnstone, the driver of the lorry, was then called. He said he had instructions to deliver a load of refreshments to Helen's Bay for a children's party, and after delivering the goods was waiting to bring back the empties.

He then explained that while he was waiting the children gathered around the lorry and begged to be taken for a drive. He also stated that one of the men in charge of the party, Mr Hamilton, asked him to take the children for a ride. He drove groups of between twenty and thirty children to Crawfordsburn and back. The lorry did the trips at between nine and eleven miles an hour. The children were cheering and singing and of course enjoying the ride. There was a steep hill with a rather sharp turn where the accident happened and as they went round the lorry gave a bit of a skid, and the side motion caused some of the children to be thrown off. Florence Gibson was killed instantly. Johnstone then stated that he pulled up and did everything he could to assist the young girl whom he brought to the home of the local doctor. The jury returned a verdict of accidental death and added that they attached no blame on the driver. But nevertheless Johnstone was said to have been haunted by the experience and felt ultimately guilty and responsible for the child's death. Of course in today's judicial system the same man would not have walked away from such an incident uncharged.

The event took place just over a 100 years ago now but the spirit of little Florence Gibson has been spotted again roaming the lonely roads of Ballymullan in County Down, and is usually spotted around the time the tragedy took place, on or around 22 June.

15

MAGGIE'S LEAP

The Mountains of Mourne, antique strange idylls
Of Maggie's Great Leap and the dread Bloody Bridge
Where thousands were slain for reading their bibles
And thrown from the parapet over the ridge.

(From 'A Poetical Description of Down', by Joseph S. Adair, 1901)

I have always wondered what this 'Bloody Bridge' was and who this 'Maggie' character was and so, with a bit of detective work and with the help of a man who dedicated his life to protecting the 'Last Leprechauns of Ireland', I got some answers. I also discovered that there is a wonderful little story all about 'Maggie's Leap'. I was given this story by a very interesting man called Kevin Woods who is a 'Leprechaun Whisperer', from Carlingford in County Louth. He was told this story by his father and grandfather who were told by their father's, grandfathers and great-grandfathers and that's how it was passed down. Mr Woods was born in 1944, and is as alive now as he was then and he often wonders why he has been so blessed.

The Bloody Bridge massacre, which took place during the Irish Rebellion of 1641, is a dark and ill-famed incident. It happened when a group of Protestant prisoners, were being taken by the Irish, under escort, from Newry to Newcastle (other accounts say Downpatrick Jail or Strangford) to be exchanged for Catholic prisoners. When they reached the old stone bridge a few miles from Newcastle, the Irish commander, Russell, received intelligence that he would be attacked at the town and that the Catholic prisoners held there had already been executed by hanging. In a fit of rage and retribution he killed some of his prisoners on the spot and drove the rest over the edge of the bridge, down to the rocks below. How many met their death's here is unclear: Adair's poem states that there were thousands of Protestant prisoners killed, some records maintain that it was a group of only ten to fifteen prisoners, while others suggest there were up to fifty were killed.

In Ulster, after hearing of the massacre, many of the Protestant settlers took their revenge by killing the native Catholic population when they got the chance, particularly in 1642-43, when a Scottish Covenanter army landed in Ulster. William Lecky, the nineteenth-century historian of the 1641 rebellion, concluded that, 'It is far from clear on which side the balance of cruelty rests'.

It was during this time of great unrest and conflict that the story of 'Maggie's Leap' took place.

Maggie was the only daughter of Deegan, a renowned and skilful poacher from Ballyvaston, Killough in County Down. His illustrious reputation and expertise was known and respected all over County Down. Salmon or pheasant, deer or hare – nothing was safe from the snares and traps laid by this crafty rustler. He was seen as a sort of Robin

Hood-type character and he always shared his spoils, feeding hungry mouths all over Newcastle and the surrounding areas. When he came into some money he was happy to hand it out to those who had none, but he was also just as happy to take it from those who had too much whenever the opportunity presented itself.

Maggie was the measure of her father's dreams and from the time she was a toddler, Deegan carried her with him on his back on his daily adventures. Before the age of ten she had mastered her father's craft and was as dexterous and competent as any of the adults in the art of poaching and knowledge of the land and all in it.

Like Redmond O'Hanlon, Maggie and her father were considered adversaries of the landed gentry and affluent residents in the area. While they were never apprehended or their identities disclosed to the authorities by the loyal country folk, they were always under suspicion. They were blamed whenever deer vanished from estates or the salmon pools of the Shimna River were fished till there was nothing left but water. The big landowners began to employ extra grounds-keepers and in some cases armed sentries. But this was to no avail for the elusive father and daughter team was never caught.

By the time Maggie was seventeen she had matured into the most beautiful and free-spirited being that had ever roamed the County of Down. She had long golden flowing curls like sunlight, eyes as blue as the sea that rolled down to the Mournes, lips like cherries and a smile that would soften even the hardest heart. She was as swift as the wind and dexterous as a butterfly. No one could outrun her or outwit her. She was a wild and wonderful creature to behold and the apple of her father's eye, who would have killed any man who dared harm a hair on her pretty head. But the destruction of wild game and fish farms in the estates forced the landlords to seek the assistance of the British Army to curtail this pillaging and plundering, particularly the poaching pair from Ballyvaston.

This new vigil carried out by the soldiers weakened Maggie and her father's resources. After a while it became almost impossible to poach the lands. Deegan himself became very disheartened by the whole affair and drew back on his activities, before long Maggie became the sole provider. Her poaching was down to a minimum but her extraordinary beauty helped her receive many gifts of food from the bored and lonely soldiers in return for a smile and a kiss on the cheek but nothing more.

One of her tricks when the time was right was to climb down the cliff face of Dundrum Bay to gather the eggs of nesting seagulls. She would fill her basket to the brim and gracefully make her way back up to the top, like a seasoned rock-climber. It was on such an excursion that she was spotted on the headland by a group of drunken soldiers. Her golden hair was blowing in the wind, her skirt tucked up for climbing, revealing her long beautiful legs as she trod elegantly along the road home with her basket full of seagull eggs. The soldiers seized their opportunity to block her path and trap her with the cliff edge behind her, and its perilous drop to the ocean below. They charged down towards her, shouting obscenities and roaring with wild drunken laughter and madness in their minds.

Maggie ran as fast she could, but she was trapped. In front of her was a great gap that lay between the cliff edge and the rest of the existing headland; if she could make it to the other side she would be free of her pursuers. The soldiers

laughed mockingly and one of them approached her menacingly stating that no human, no matter how pretty, could make it to the other side unless they sprouted wings. Maggie could not swim but death by drowning or crashing onto the rocks below seemed a better fate compared to what the brutal soldiers had in mind for her. Still holding on to the basket of eggs, she took a deep breath and called upon all the powers of the universe that had protected her up until this point, then turned and leaped to freedom. Amazingly she landed with grace and dexterity on the other side, leaving her tormentors standing with their eyes and mouths wide-open, looking completely astonished and bewildered. One of the soldiers went to fire his musket at her but the senior member of the group ordered him to put his gun down, stating that such a magnificent and fearless creature should never be harmed for fear of punishment from God himself. Legend has it that not a single egg was broken and they all lay unharmed in her basket.

Apparently Maggie continued on for many years, providing food for her father and those who were too weak to help themselves. Sadly for every red-blooded male of the time she never married or left behind any children to carry on her legacy. Nevertheless, she is still remembered in County Down by the chasm she cleared north of Newcastle still known to this day as Maggie's Leap.

16

THE LISBURN GIANT

There are still residents in Lisburn, Blaris, and Hillsborough who recollect Charley Hamilton. That remarkable man was a native of Sprucefield, and worked at the building now occupied by a branch of the Hilden Flax and Thread Works. At the time referred to, it was a damask-bleaching concern under the proprietorship of William, Walter, and James Coulson. Charley worked many years as a millwright in the employment of these gentlemen, but his claim to fame was his extreme height and the athletic feats he could perform.

On one occasion he had been engaged by Messrs Bradshaw & Moreland, of the Hillsborough Distillery, to construct a water-wheel, the diameter of which very much exceeded the largest ever made in Ulster. Many people came to see this monster of mechanism, and on the day it was finished the Marquis of Downshire arrived at the spot. His lordship seemed anxious to see the wheel turn on its axis, and said he would send to the park for half-a-dozen stout men to move the great machine. 'Beg your pardon, my lord', said Charley, taking off the cap he usually wore while at work, 'you need not get any aid of your people, I can turn the wheel myself,' and stretching out his brawny arms he astounded both the peer and the people by setting in motion the immense machine, which he did with as much ease as an ordinary man could trundle a wheelbarrow.

In his twenty-second year Charley Hamilton could stretch out his right arm on a chair, and, a person of twelve stone weight having stood on his hand, he would raise him up as high as the ceiling permitted, and carry the person round the room, still keeping the arm straight out from the shoulder.

For several years in his early adult life Charley was engaged by an itinerant showman and travelled through the principal counties in England and Scotland, exhibiting himself as the Giant of Ulster in the chief cities and towns of each country. His height, according to the show's posters, was eight feet four inches (which in truth was about four inches more than his natural dimension). He was a man of considerable intelligence, and his experience of the world did much to educate him. In the summer of 1820 Charley Hamilton was being exhibited at Edinburgh and had the honour of appearing before Sir Walter Scott, Professor Wilson, the 'Christopher North' of Blackwood; Francis Jeffrey, of the Edinburgh Review; Hogg, the Ettrick Shepherd, and other literary lions. On Sunday morning, whilst taking a stroll through the streets of Edinburgh in the very early hours (when very few people would likely be astir), Charley decided to light his pipe, so he stopped under one of the old oil lamps, and, stretching up his arm, lifted off the top and set fire to a slip of paper he held in his hand. It was about six o'clock, and through the grey mist of a June dawn a number of journeymen tailors, who

were corkscrewing their way home after Saturday night's symposium, having seen the strange sight, made the best of their way to the place and set up a lusty cheer, as they gazed on the ample proportions of the giant, who rapidly retreated to his caravan.

When Charley retired from the show business life he returned to his native Lisburn and his millwright trade. He married and had several children, though none exceeded the ordinary size of those around them. Like all giants he died young, but for years he was fondly remembered for his amiable disposition, kindly spirit and his ringing laugh, which was as hearty as that of a schoolboy on his holiday.

17

THE SOLEMN DEATH
OF BERNARD MCCANN

J. Temple Reilly of Scarvagh House recorded this great folk story,
which is a melancholic tale of murder and retribution in County
Down over 150 years ago.

When Temple was visiting in Galway, in September 1862, a
respectable-looking man accosted him, and addressing him
by name, asked if he knew him.

Temple replied, 'No, I do not. Who are you?'

'Oh,' said he, 'I'm Hughes. Sure, your father hanged my
father.'

Several versions have been given of the events that
led to Hughes senior's death, but the following account
is understood to have been drawn up from the most
authentic sources, many of the statements contained in
the narrative having been taken from the lips of persons
who were personally cognizant of the facts now fully
detailed.

In July 1810, a young man named Bernard McCann
sought employment as a journeyman baker in Lisburn. He was

a native of Newtownhamilton, in which town he had served an apprenticeship to that trade; and after a few days' search for work, he found employment with John Woods, then the leading trader engaged in the business in Lisburn. McCann was rather a fine-looking lad of about eighteen years of age. He had got a fair education for a young fellow of his class, and was considered a superior hand in the higher branches of the manufacture of bread. After some months' service with Mr Woods, he left for another house in the same trade, owned by Adam Sloan, where he continued for nearly three years.

In those days the County of Louth was famed, as it has been to the present, for the superior breeds of horses, and a jockey named Owen McAdam engaged in the sale of colts and fillies, which he brought from thence to the north-east districts of Ulster. He had disposed of this string of animals at the July fair in Lisburn, and, as the Maze Races for that year (1813) were then in full swing, he made a detour in his journey to his farm near Dundalk, for the purpose of spending a day on the race-ground and enjoying the sport. On arrival at the course he met Barney McCann, and, finding him a chatty, agreeable companion, he invited his new acquaintance into one of the tents, where the pair drank pretty freely.

Owen McAdam was a shrewd man of business, but in other respects was as simple and unsuspecting as a mere child. While enjoying his grog he had much talk about Lisburn, and said he had to go back to that town to get the price of a colt he had sold there. McCann said that he worked in Lisburn, and offered to accompany him thither. They walked on the way together, the dealer leading his pony.

On arriving to the town Owen called on his customer and received the sum due him, and, with McCann, adjourned to a public house, where they had more liquor. During the short time they were in that house the horse dealer produced a large role of bank notes, and adding to it the money he had just received, he secured the whole amount in a leather bag, and placed the parcel in the ample pocket of his great coat. McCann had never before looked upon such a number of bank notes, and, as it was afterwards supposed by those who had known him as trustworthy, that the temptation to possess himself of the money were too strong to be resisted.

After their drink the horse dealer again mounted his pony, saying he would ride to Hillsborough and stop there for the night. McCann offered to accompany him part of the way, and as they arrived at a roadside public house, kept by a man named James Roney, they got more whisky, and on that occasion the greater part of the whole was drunk by McAdam, his companion only taking a very small share. It was then ten o'clock, and almost dark, and the horse dealer had refreshed himself so freely that he could barely keep his seat on the saddle. McCann walked by the pony's head, and it was observed by persons who saw them passing that, instead of taking the coach road, they went round a by-lane that led to the banks of Lagan River.

Nothing further was heard of the horse dealer until the succeeding Sunday morning, when the body of a man was seen floating in the canal. On its being brought to the bank it was at once recognised as that of the person who had last been seen in company with the baker. A coroner's inquest was held on Monday, and in the course of the investigation several witnesses proved that the deceased and Barney McCann had spent the Friday together at the Maze Course, and drank very freely in more than one of the refreshment tents. James Roney stated that the man whose body had been found in the canal was the person with whom the baker called at the door of his public house at ten o'clock on the previous Friday night, that McCann paid for a naggin of whisky, drank a small part of it himself, and gave the remainder to a man who sat outside on his pony. The evidence fully corroborated the fact that the deceased had a considerable sum of money in his possession, and a silver watch, all of which had been carried off.

McCann had disappeared, and, after due deliberation, the jury returned a verdict of murder against him, and a warrant was issued for his apprehension. In the meantime the greatcoat of the poor man who had lost his life was taken to Lisburn and hung up on the church gate, in the hope of discovering the relatives of the deceased, and the body was placed in a coffin, but the lid remained loose on it, so any potential relatives could check the man's features. During the week an old man and his son, who had come in search of the horse dealer arrived in Lisburn, and when they saw the coat, they were overcome with grief. One of those men was Owen McAdam's father, and the other his brother. The coffin and the remains were conveyed to Louth for interment in the family burial-ground.

We may here state that the banks of the canal, near which the body of the horse dealer was found, showed foot-marks suggesting a serious struggle, and numerous people, led by curiosity, went to look at the scene of the supposed murder.

During the next week it was discovered that the baker McCann and two other persons had dined in Hillsborough, and that he paid the bill with a banknote which he took from a bulky parcel. This was on Saturday, after the night's carokuse, and as the body of his victim had not then been discovered no one questioned where McCann had got the money. From thence he rode the grey pony to a place near Portadown, and tried to sell it, but, failing to do so, he left the animal with a farmer, saying if he gave it a month's grass he would be back at that time, and pay him for the pasture. Ireland had not any trained police in those days, and the warrant for the suspected murderer having been placed in the hands of two county constables, these worthy officers searched about for weeks, gazing suspiciously in the faces of every young man who was at all like the description given of McCann; but their mission was in vain, and at length even the dark deed had been all but forgotten.

Galway, the maritime capital of Connaught, famed in the western section of Ireland as the 'City of the Tribes', was at one time bustling with the traffic of Spanish wine merchants, and there may still be seen there a few older buildings which are said to have been erected by some of the settlers from the land of the olive who became residents in the days of Queen Elizabeth I. Nor is it just in the castellated turrets and peculiarly arched entrances which characterise the architecture of those buildings that the visitor to Galway sees evidences of Continentalism; but there may be observed in the handsome countenances of some brunettes many of the distinguishing features of the Spanish maiden. In that ocean-washed city there resided, in 1823, John Hughes, a prosperous butcher and much-respected dealer in cattle. By the course of industry, great attention to worldly affairs, and a popular manner, he had amassed property, and married the daughter of a respectable trader, with whom he lived very happily. From whence John Hughes had come when he first entered the City of Galway not one of his neighbours inquired: it was enough to know he was a good member of society, peaceable and well-disposed in his walk through life, and as such every true-born Celt received their new friend with a *céade míle fáilte*.

There was at that time in our history a race of itinerant pedlars, who travelled through Ireland, some of them from the far north to the extreme points of the south and west. They traded in all varieties of soft goods, silk stockings and cotton shawls, printed dress patterns and other haberdasheries, and, like all business people throughout the ages, they delighted in long profits. Carrying on their shoulders their entire stock of goods, which they usually made up in a canvas pack, they trudged through the country, armed with an oaken stick, which did duty as a walking-staff as well as a yard-measure. These sturdy dealers could have travelled twenty or thirty miles a day, stopping on route at farmhouses, where they usually found ready purchasers. One of the tribe to which we refer had often met the young baker, who was charged with the death of the horse dealer, and while journeying through the County of Down, and immediately after the occurrence, he had heard much gossip and no end of details respecting it. In June 1823, he was in the West of Ireland for the first time, and paid a visit to Galway. Passing down William Street in that ancient city he was asked, in a bantering style, by John Hughes if he would buy a joint of meat. His interrogator's tone of voice and peculiar cast of features appeared almost to startle him. He peered into the face of Hughes, and seemed to be collecting in his mind recollections of ten years before. After some chaffing, during which the Galway man did not appear to exhibit any symptom of having met the pedlar before, the latter passed down the street saying, 'Well, you may hear from me again.'

John L. Reilly, collector of customs at the port of Galway, was also a Justice of the Peace for the county. On the morning after his interview with John Hughes, the pedlar called at the Custom House, and requested one of the officials be good enough to say to Mr Reilly that a stranger wished to see him on magisterial business. He was immediately shown into a private office, and, on the collector making his appearance, he told that gentleman he had criminal information against the cattle-dealer who called himself John Hughes. The magistrate appeared quite astounded.

'There is no more respectable man in Galway than Mr Hughes,' he said, 'and unless you can show me that you have strong grounds for suspicion – in fact, something like certainty – I would hesitate in taking your information.'

'I feel perfectly assured I am right, and beg to tell your Worship that the man's name is not Hughes, but Barney McCann, a baker, who nearly ten years ago was charged with the robbery and murder of a cattle-dealer named Owen McAdam, at a place called Blaris, near Hillsborough,' said the pedlar, in the tone of one who knew well what he was saying.

'My brother, Mr Edmund Reilly, resides in that town,' replied the magistrate. 'He is agent for the Marquis of Downshire, and one of the county justices. I shall write him and ascertain the facts, such as may have come to his knowledge.'

'Your Worship may act as you think best in that case, but I respectfully insist on swearing information,' and as the pedlar said this he stood before the magistrate in the most determined attitude.

Mr Reilly then stated that he would send for the accused, and a messenger having been despatched for that purpose, John Hughes shortly afterwards arrived with the officer, and was confronted with his accuser.

A momentary change passed over the countenance of the man as he met the keen glance of the pedlar, but speedily regaining his self-possession, he begged with great respect to know what might be his Worship's pleasure in sending for him.

Mr Reilly said a very grave charge had been made against him by the person there present, and that previous to issuing a warrant he had sent for him, that he might learn the nature of the accusation.

The pedlar stood quite cool as Mr Hughes flatly denied the charge; and in very emphatic terms he reiterated the story he had told the magistrates; and, having done so, he turned round, and looking the accused full in the face, continued: 'Barney McCann, I now charge you solemnly as being the man who robbed and murdered Owen McAdam, and afterwards threw his body into the Lagan River.'

The accused had by that time grown into a very powerful man, with muscular strength equal to almost any emergency. Had he wished to escape he could have felled at one blow either of the two that stood before him, and fought his way through the clerks and subordinates in the customs office; he, however, listened to the serious statement made against him with all the coolness of conscious innocence, and merely said: 'I have never been in either Lisburn or Hillsborough, and until yesterday evening do not recollect having seen this person who makes the charge against me.'

Mr Reilly could only repeat that he felt great reluctance to take the information. He hoped Mr Hughes would be able to prove his innocence of the charge but in the meantime it would be his painful duty to send him to prison. Nothing could have exceeded the astonishment, and, indeed, the real sorrow that prevailed in Galway when the report spread that Mr John Hughes had been charged with murder. He was the last person on whom those who knew him best would have laid such an accusation, and his practical philanthropy and private benevolence had been so general that no one had the slightest idea of his guilt. A great number of people had by that time assembled before the Custom House and a couple of police having arrived, John Hughes was removed to prison followed by the crowd, each member of which looked on the affair as one of mistaken identity. So great, however, was popular indignation aroused against the informant that, had he not make his escape, he would have been seized upon and flung into the deepest waters of the Claddagh.

In the course of a few days, Mr Reilly received a reply from his brother, the agent of the Downshire estates, and in that letter full corroboration was given of all the statements made about Barney McCann. The only question to be tried was as to whether that person and John Hughes were one and the same individual. A warrant was therefore made out for the removal of the prisoner from Galway to the jail of Downpatrick, and John Hunter, a constable from Hillsborough, was despatched to execute the same.

On his arrival in Galway arrangements were immediately made for the prisoner to be handed over to the constable, and for that purpose seats were taken in the mail coach from thence to Dublin. Hughes was handcuffed, and also chained by the ankles, and a large cloak provided by Mr Reilly was thrown over him, so that as he sat beside the constable the manacles could not be seen by the other inside passengers. Compared with the physique of his prisoner, Mr Hunter seemed a mere lad, and in later life he often alluded to the fears of personal violence he had entertained in the course of that eventful journey. While the travellers passed that part of the way which included the run from Ballinasloe to Athlone, they had the inside of the coach to themselves, and there again Hughes had his chance of escape, as, even fettered as he was, he could have knocked Hunter senseless, and opened the coach door and got clear off; but he never showed the least disposition to get free. On the contrary, he chatted in friendly terms with his keeper, and when they reached Dublin he jumped out of the vehicle on the street opposite the Post office as if neither chain nor strap had bound him.

Next day the constable and his prisoner travelled by mail to Hillsborough, and when set down at the Corporation Arms, Hughes looked over the streets and made inquiries about the town with all the nonchalance of a perfect stranger. Many people, knowing that the supposed murderer would likely arrive, had assembled about the hotel door to catch a view of his person. Mr Hunter, however, had the unfortunate man taken to his own house, where refreshments were liberally supplied for him previous to his conveyance to the County Jail at Downpatrick. All this time the prisoner never lost his hopefulness, and spoke freely of being able to get clear of the charge. As he left the constable's house, he thanked that officer's wife for her kindness to him, adding that he would call on her, as he would be going home after the trial, and tender his acknowledgements in a more fitting way than he could then do.

McCann, as we may now call him, lay for seven weeks in jail before the assizes began. And in the course of that time he made friends with all the officials, from the governor down to the lowest subordinate, every one of whom entertained the hope of his acquittal.

The case was tried by Judge Moore, and two of the ablest counsels on the North East circuit were retained for the defence. On his being brought into the dock the crowd in the court turned to gaze on the prisoner, who appeared to be a powerful man of about thirty years of age, rather above the middle height, and evidently above fifteen stone in weight. He wore the prison dress, but that outer mode of clothing did not conceal his calm and self-possessed appearance.

Strangely the pedlar who accused the arrest of the accused did not appear at the trial. On the part of the Crown, every possible exertion had been made to collect evidence for the prosecution. It was proved by James Roney, the owner of the public house at which the prisoner and McAdam got their last refreshment, that Barney McCann, the man on his trail, had paid for two glasses of whiskey, that he drunk about half a one of them himself, and forced the other on a man who was outside the door, mounted on a grey pony. The same witness added that he watched the two turning off the main road and passing down the narrow way that led to the banks of the Lagan river. A watchmaker of Newtownhamilton, Barney McCann's birth-place, proved that on 30 July 1813, the prisoner, whom he recognised notwithstanding the great change in his appearance, left a watch with him to repair (and which he produced in court). It was a peculiar watch, with the figures of four soldiers on the dial-plate, and it was afterwards proved to have been the property of the deceased horse dealer. Another witness, who lived near Portadown, stated that on Monday, 29 July 1813 the prisoner, whose name he did not then know, offered to sell him a grey pony, which he refused, and that some time afterwards the pony was claimed by a brother of the horse dealer who said it was formerly used by deceased.

Several persons testified to having seen the young baker McCann and the deceased McAdam at the Maze races on the afternoon of Friday 26 July, and a Lisburn publican told of seeing a roll of bank notes in the hands of the horse dealer. The owner of the hotel in Hillsborough, in whose place McCann and two other men had dinner, on Saturday 27 July, observed an immense number of bank notes in the hands of the person who was then in the dock, who also offered to sell him a curious-faced watch for ten shillings, a watch he believed to have been the same as that shown in court that day. Counsel for the accused cross-examined each of the witnesses, and appealed to the jury was it likely that a man who had for ten years borne the highest character as a quiet, well-to-do citizen would be guilty of the enormities with which he had been charged. Nothing, however, could be brought forward to shake the testimony of the man that gave evidence for the prosecution.

The case having been closed by all sides, Judge Moore proceeded to give his charge to the jury. His lordship had taken copious notes of the evidence, and in the course of his address, which occupied two hours, he alluded to the high character borne by the prisoner during his residence in Galway, and the valuable testimonial he had received from the collector of customs at that port. In recapping the evidence, the learned judge dwelt at some length on the testimony of James Roney, the man who kept the public house at a country place called the Warren Gate, and distant about ten minutes' walk from the scene of the murder. Roney had not only sworn positively to the prisoner as being the person that called at his house with the deceased, but added that the prisoner only took a small portion of the naggin of whiskey he had paid for, and gave the remainder to the man on horseback, who had already had too much liquor. It was true, the judge said, that the case for the Crown rested solely on circumstantial evidence, but in the whole course of his experience he had never heard a more sustained line of concurrent testimony. The case, however, would now go to the jury, and if, after what had been laid before them, any doubt rested on their minds as to the prisoner at the bar being the identical Bernard McCann, they should give him the full benefit of that doubt.

The jury retired, and during their absence from the court a perfect silence prevailed; even the people in the gallery seemed impressed with the dread solemnity of the occasion. McCann stood in the front of the dock, looking calm, as had been his wont from the very commencement of the trial; but when the door of the jurors room was opened, and when not the slightest whisper could have been heard, a slight flush passed over his countenance. However, he quickly regained his former spirit of composure, and when the twelve men on whose fate his life rested were once again in their box he gazed around him as though he had been an ordinary spectator.

'How say you, gentlemen – is the prisoner guilty or not guilty?' inquired the Clerk of the Crown.

'Guilty,' replied the foreman, handing up the paper containing the fatal decision. As he pronounced the word a low wail of sorrow rose from amid the densely packed audience, as if in that single term the death-knell of some dear friend and been rung out.

Judge Moore put on the black cap, with the most intense stillness reigning throughout the court, and the deep feeling with which his lordship delivered the terrible sentence seemed to have had its influence on all within the sound of his voice. As he wound up with the usual prayer, 'May the Lord have mercy on your soul,' he sank back on the judgement seat, and, covering his face with the official robe, was for some minutes quite overcome by the terrible drama.

It had been supposed that during the ten days which intervened between the passing of the sentence and the time appointed for its execution the condemned man would make some confession of his guilt, but not a word was heard from him on the subject. With the governor of the jail he talked freely about his wife and children, mourning over the terrible stain which his death at the hands of the hangman would inflict on his family. He spoke with feeling of all who were near and dear to him, still keeping at a distance any approach to the incidents of his early life. Even when in private conversation with his spiritual adviser, Bernard McCann was reticent; he alluded in grateful terms to the attention and kindness he had received from all the officers connected with the prison, and in their turn those people entertained the greatest sympathy towards him.

The execution took place on 7 August, and that scene was melancholy beyond ordinary conception. On that morning an immense crowd was assembled in front of Downpatrick Jail, completely filling the large space opposite to that portion of the prison where, in those days, 'the drop' or gallows had been placed. This engine of death was fixed on the jail wall, about fifteen feet above the level of the pathway. It consisted of an iron grating hinged against the side of the prison, where it hung in ordinary times, but when an execution was about to take place it was raised up so as to be on a level with the outer doors of the press-room. McCann had slept pretty well the night before that fateful morning, and when the governor visited him in the condemned cell

to inquire what he would have for breakfast, he replied that
he would not eat anything. His clergyman, who had arrived,
urged him to have some refreshment, but he again refused,
and at the same time apologised for his conduct in the
case by saying, 'I am sure your reference will put the most
charitable construction on the conduct of a fellow creature
who is on the very brink of eternity. I have no desire for
food.' A small glass of brandy was then brought him; he
took part of it, and afterwards begged permission of the
others present that for a few minutes he might have a private
interview with his clergyman. The request was granted, and
about six minutes before eight o'clock the subsheriff of the
county and the governor of the jail, with their subordinates,
entered the cell, and the governor announced that the time
of the execution had almost arrived.

The subsheriff then made the formal demand that the
body of Bernard McCann be delivered up to him. That sad
ceremonial had some effect on the culprit, and he winced
a little at the transfer, but in a second was himself again.
A procession, headed by the clergyman, was then formed,
and all those present passed on slowly in the direction of
the press-room, the spiritual attendant reading the prayers
of his Church, to which McCann responded with seeming
fervour. Arrived at the fatal apartment, the executioner
made his first appearance, the prison bell tolled dismally,
and the grim official proceeded with the pinioning process,
fastening the prisoner's arms with a strong leather strap
passed over his elbows and buckled tightly at his back.
McCann was then conducted out of the door that opened
above the street, and immediately under which was the
great platform. As soon as he appeared the cry, 'Hats off!'
was heard in low tones from various sections of the crowd

in front of the jail, and immediately every man in that vast assembly stood with his head uncovered; but, with the exception of the cry alluded to, not even a whisper could have been heard.

In the meantime the governor and the subsheriff stood close by while the hangman fastened another strap round the unfortunate man's ankles, and during that final preparation the latter looked for a moment on the sea of upturned faces as it surged and swayed like a heaving mass in the street below. He then cast a hasty glance at the beam, from which dangled the ominous rope, with its peculiar noose, right above the treacherous iron grating, and within a few inches of the top of his head. Having parted with the clergyman, who had been fairly overcome by his feeling, and shaken hands with the governor and turnkeys, the white cap was tied under the unfortunate man's chin and the rope adjusted round his neck; the executioner stepped back and, withdrawing the bolt that upheld the drop, the culprit fell, but, whether from his great weight or form some neglect on the part of the authorities, the rope broke, and the wretched culprit was precipitated into the street.

Terrible indeed was the feeling of popular indignation aroused by that sad incident, and had some of the excited people in the crowd been able to lay hands on the subsheriff, who was charged with neglect in not having provided a stronger rope, he would have been severely handled. A troop of soldiers had been placed on guard at that portion of the street which lay immediately below the gallows, and rushing forward they raised McCann and placed him on the rude blaey coffin, which had been left there as the receptacle for his remains. It was marvellous that he did not seem injured by the fall. There was an old tradition, believed in by the people in many parts of Ireland, that in case of any person being condemned for execution, should there be a mischance in the carrying out of the sentence, and by which the criminal escapes death from the time being, he cannot again be subjected to the fatal ordeal, but should get free. Under the idea that the tradition was correct, McCann had no sooner been set on the lid of his own coffin than he cried out, 'My life's my own.' Many in the crowd agreed, and, rushing past the guard of soldiers, some men pulled the white cap from off the poor fellow's face. Several glasses of water were handed him, and he eagerly drank their contents. The governor, who seemed deeply affected at the sad affair, then told McCann that he must again submit to the sentence.

Fortunately for himself and for his personal safety, the subsheriff had not occasion to appear in the crowd, but his men procured another rope, and in about half an hour the ghastly arrangements were again completed. McCann's ankles were unbound, and he was led round to the door of the jail; and although strapped so tightly by the arms he ascended the flight of steps that led to the press-room with the agility of a boy. When placed once more on the 'drop' he appeared to dread another fall more than death itself, and he anxiously appealed to the governor in the words, 'For God's sake see that the rope is strong enough this time.'

The executioner then came forward, and again accomplished his horrid preliminary work. The drop fell, and Barney McCann passed into the unseen world amid a sense of sorrow and sympathy never equalled on any similar occasion. Many were of opinion that, under all the circumstances, the life of the chief actor might well have been spared. No doubt a terrible crime had been committed;

but only God knows the secrets of all hearts could tell how deep had been the repentance of the perpetrator from that terrible night at the canal bank, when he first robbed Owen McAdam, took his victim's life, and cast his body into the river. He had become a well-conducted and highly respected citizen, and as punishment never yet proved a deterring influence when public sympathy was all on the side of the sufferer, justice might well have given way to the higher attribute of mercy in the case of Bernard McCann.

18

BLACK DERMOD

This story was recorded in the Banbridge Almanac *of 1880 by an anonymous writer. It is a powerful and beautiful County Down folk tale and wonderful addition to this collection. The story was also known as 'The Half-Brothers'. The original was somewhat disjointed, so I took it upon myself to piece it together. I hope you enjoy it.*

The County of Down is a district renowned for its varied picturesque scenery and general interest. It is a pleasant spot for a summer ramble that could not be easily found elsewhere. No matter whether the traveller's taste prefers the rugged scenery of the uplands that border Dundrum Bay, the grandeur of Strangford Lough with over 360 inlets, its ruined castles and powerful currents. No matter if one may travel in pursuit of pleasure, health, pilgrimage, information or the picturesque and antique splendour of round towers, ancient buildings or Druidic remains and other archaeological treasures so common in the County, no one will be disappointed.

This story features one such rambler and his experience that is surely one of wonder in the magical County of Down. I know

*very little of this character, only that Ireland was the birthplace
of his mother's race. It is not specified where he himself was
living at the time; one can only assume it was the mainland of
Great Britain as he states he paid numerous visits to Ireland for
hiking or rambling excursions on its shores. He was stopping off
to visit some friends in the village of Rostrevor, which lies at the
foot of Slieve Ban, and this is where his story begins.*

One morning our rambler left to go on a walk with his
friend Charlie Vernon, whom he was staying with. They
crossed the Bay of Kilkeel and began a trip around the coast
to Newcastle. They intended to rest for the night and make
an ascent of Slieve Donard, the Monarch of the Mournes,
the next morning. In the evening they amused themselves
by strolling about the beach, watching the fishing boats
that lay at anchor in the bay with their sails flapping lazily
against their masts, while their owners got ready to tempt
the dangers of the deep.

Whilst admiring the boats, the rambler's friend gave
a startled cry and pointed towards a narrow ledge that
jutted out from the side of the mountain overhanging the
sea. On the precipice two men were engaged in a violent
struggle. One of the men stumbled and ended up hanging,
suspended over the raging sea. He was holding on with only
one hand and was reaching out for assistance with the other.
His opponent walked towards him and brought his boot
down hard on the poor man's hand. He fell screaming and
the dark waters swallowed him up below.

According to the narrator of this tale, he and his friend
ran as fast as they could to get a boat and save the drowning
man. But they were stopped in their tracks by an elderly
gentleman who happened to be the parish priest of the

area and introduced himself as Father Michael. 'Ah Sirs!' exclaimed the old man 'It is of no use; the struggle that you have witnessed was not between mortal men. Every year, on this day, the same tragedy is played out again and again'. As you can imagine the two young men were confused and disbelieving of this statement. The old priest asked them to sit down on some large stones near them and calm themselves, and he would tell them of this tragic tale.

Father Michael began, 'You see, this all began twenty-five years ago, when two brothers struggled on the brink of that abyss. Afterwards the one who hurled the other into the sea committed suicide, and since that time, on the anniversary of his death, the villagers have been terrified by the sight that you have just witnessed'. By this time a number of fishermen had assembled around Father Michael and the two walkers, and all wholeheartedly agreed with what the priest said. The old-priest then asked the two ramblers to dine at his cottage and even offered to be their guide up the mountain the next day. He promised them that he would tell them the whole story of the apparition during their walk. Of course the two men accepted without a second thought. They ate tasty bacon and cabbage at the priest's house and even partook in some of his stash of the 'Rare Auld Mountain Dew', better known as 'Poteen'. Father Michael was a kind and educated man with a wealth of knowledge about the area and the mountain range. He was a dignified and vigorous-looking character with a shock of grey hair that sat on his head like a wiry bird's nest. His face was well etched with lines and a pair of spectacles framed deep knowing eyes that sparkled with wisdom. They left his abode happy and content and the following morning met Father Michael there, again waiting for them, ready to ascend the mountain.

The ascent of Slieve Donard is a gradual one of about
four miles, climbing nearly 3,000 feet above sea level.
There is a mountain path winding up the rock-strewn
slopes and scattered bog-land. To the left of the mountain
lies Ardglass and Strangford Lough, which Father Michael
pointed out was part of the story he had promised to tell his
companions. At last they reached the summit and, throwing
themselves on the grass, they gazed long and earnestly on the
surrounding landscape. Near the summit they saw the ruins
of two buildings that the priest identified as being the cell
and oratory of St Donard, a disciple of St Patrick, who once
made his home on the mountains; and here the peasantry
assembles on the patron saint's day to do penance and pay
their devotions. Here, sitting at the foot of the ruins, Father
Michael began his tale.

He pointed towards one of the mountains and said, 'You
see, gentlemen, the mountain that stands on the south-west,
divided from Slieve Donard by that narrow vale and stream?
It is called 'Slieve Snaven', or 'The Creeping Mountain',
because a portion of it can only be ascended in a creeping
posture. As you can see, it resembles some old fortification,
very high, over-hanging and detached, as it were, from the
eastern side of the mountain. After the rain a stream rushes
from the western side of the rock, shooting from the top
and falling in a large cascade to the beach; to the east of
this fall there is a vast natural cave, with an entrance nearly
as wide as the cave itself. This chamber is lined with ferns,
grass and beautiful mountain plants and is inhabited by
many hundreds of hawks, jackdaws and owls. At the far end
there are some crevices through which light penetrates, and
if you climb up through a narrow passage on the left, to the
top of the rock, you will arrive at one of the most beautiful,

magnificent and romantic spots that can well be conceived'. Father Michael stood up for a minute and took a swig from the bottle he had brought with him and then offered it to his comrades, who accepted happily. They were all happy and content, enjoying the calmness and serenity of the situation. Father Michael sat back down and continued his story.

'One summer evening over twenty-five years ago two lovers were seated there side by side. The young man was called Carrick O'Farrell and the young woman was called Nelly O'Hara', when the priest said this girl's name his eyes glazed over and there was a sorrow about him. He began again, 'Everybody loved Nelly O'Hara; she was the prettiest girl in County Down, a county noted for the beauty of its women, I'll have you know,' stated the old priest, smiling. At a dance everybody was ready to fight for the honour of shaking a foot with her; indeed rival wooers did often finish by breaking each others heads in revenge for their own broken hearts, till at last it was well understood that the only one Nelly was ever going to be interested in was young Carrick O'Farrell. He was the son of a small farmer who lived near Kilkeel, he was a fine lad, who could hold his own and could handle a blackthorn-stick with the best of them. One by one they retired from the contest, and the little world on the Down coast accepted that he was the chosen suitor.

But everything was not all roses and love, for Nelly's poor father, Denis O'Hara, had met with many misfortunes. During the early part of the potato famine, he had become security for a poorer neighbour, who had since failed, and the little money Denis had saved soon disappeared. The rent, which up to this period had been punctually paid, fell into arrears; his landlord, a stern and harsh man, who had no compassion for his tenants, threatened to turn him out of his farm. Ruin seemed to stare Denis O'Hara in the face. Then, for the first time in his life, he was forced to do something that would take the light out of his beautiful daughter's eyes, the one thing he loved more than anything else in the world. He refused his consent for her to marry the one she loved, Carrick O'Farrell.

Poor handsome Carrick was not the eldest son; his father had been twice married and had two children. Carrick had an older half-brother called Dermod, he was a morose and menacing character and he was strongly suspected by the villagers of being the cause of several wrecks that had taken place around the time. False lights had been used, and the vessels were lured to certain destruction among the treacherous rocks that studded the shores of Strangford Harbour. Although there was no solid proof of the culprit, rumour pointed to the dark, sombre man who answered to the name 'Dermod Dhu', meaning 'Black Dermod'.

Black Dermod was one of the many suitors who had been rejected by Nelly, but unlike the others he had not given up all hope. He advanced small sums of money, from time to time, to Nelly's father, and when he found out that Denis was in dire straits and in need of financial aid, he once more began to urge his position of Nelly's suitor. The father soon consented, but Nelly, who despised and feared Dermod as much as she loved and worshiped his half-brother, declared that nothing should tempt her break her promise to Carrick.

Father Michel stopped and looked at his two companions and asked if he was boring them with his story. They both replied that they were intrigued, even enchanted and urged him to carry on. The priest solemnly nodded and continued with his tale.

'Well as we know, the constant dripping of water will, in time, wear away a rock; and at last Dermod swore that if Nelly did not marry him, he would send her father to prison. She knew the shame would kill her father, begged for a month's delay, and promised to become, at the end of that time, the wife of the man who would pay all her father's debts and prevent him from being turned out of the home of his forefathers.

Nelly arranged to meet her lover Carrick at the place that Father Michael had pointed out to comrades earlier that day. This spot had long been their meeting place, but now the gloomy mountain seemed to frown upon their fortunes and love, casting a shadow over their happiness. Their situation was bleak, but there was still a chance that Carrick could solve their predicament. Nelly had bought them time by asking for the month's grace. That meant that Carrick could call in a favour that may save them. He would have to go to Dublin to meet a man whose yacht he had saved from wreckage on the rocks, as it was following the false beacons left by his cruel half-brother. They parted sadly and Nelly prayed as she had never done before that her lover would be successful in his task.'

Father Michael propped himself up and excitedly told his companions how Carrick had saved the yacht. 'A few months previous, Carrick had spotted a beautiful cutter-yacht, with the stars and stripes flying at her masthead. She was the property of an American gentleman called Mr Winthrop, who was making a tour around the coastline of Ireland. He was accompanied by his daughter Kate and a party of friends. They had docked a few times around the coast and climbed the Mourne Mountains and taken many of the walks round about. But about a week after the yacht's arrival she was caught up in a terrible storm and, it being night time, the crew on board could not make out where the harbour was. Black Dermod had placed burning beacons along the rocks, hoping that the boat with its wealthy crew and bountiful cargo would be smashed and he would benefit from the spoils. The roar of the wind and the billowing waves had the young Kate Winthrop terrified. She was screaming so, that her shrieks could be heard above the waves. As the vessel seemed doomed to certain destruction, a fishing hooker passed under her stern and a voice was heard hailing her. A rope was thrown and a man hauled on board. He sprang to the wheel and just as the man at the look-out cried 'Breakers Ahead!' he roared his command: 'Haul your starboard braces! And ease off to port!' Well the sailors rushed to obey and the yacht answering, her helm swung round and entered a narrow channel with breakers on both sides of it. For a few minutes, which felt like an eternity she held her course, and then her passage widened and, like an ocean bird, she rounded the point and reached the open sea. The worst of the danger was over and after a while the gale and tempestuous waves slackened. The cutter was safely anchored in Strangford Harbour; those on board owing their lives to Carrick O'Farrell were in deep gratitude to the young man.

Mr Winthrop was by no means ungrateful to the young man; he offered him a farm back in America. But Carrick preferred to stay at home and there was no way he would leave without Nelly. He knew that she would not desert her father in his troubles. However, Mr Winthrop told him he would give him time to reflect upon his offer, and said he would be staying in Dublin for the next few months and would write to him on his arrival.

So with this in mind, Carrick made his way to the capital city to meet the kind American and tell him of the terrible predicament he and his beloved Nelly were in. When he met Mr Winthrop and told him all, without hesitation Winthrop gave him enough money to not only pay off old O'Hara's debts but leave Carrick himself enough to start afresh. Winthrop then offered to bring Carrick back to Dundrum on board the yacht; telling him the whole party wished to be present at his wedding, and that he still hoped to persuade him to cross the Atlantic with his new bride. The cutter made a quick passage and was soon anchored in the bay. Carrick thanked his friends and made his way towards Slieve Donard. Before he would go to Nelly's cottage he was determined to climb the hillside and look once more at the old meeting place where they had parted so sorrowfully a few days before.

Well he did so and was met there by none other than his wicked half-brother, Dermod Dhu. 'So you have returned then?' said Dermod, mockingly. 'Yes and with great success!' shouted Carrick. 'I have returned just in time to prevent the villainy you have plotted. I have the money to release Dennis O'Hara.'

'Liar!' roared Dermod.

Carrick replied with a light, satisfied laugh as he turned and began to descend down the cliff. Hoping to take him at a disadvantage, Dermod sprang up at him and seized him by the throat. The two brothers were equally matched in regards to height and strength, but the younger brother's clean style of living gave him advantage over his insalubrious brother. As they struggled they drew closer and closer to the smooth and slippery edge of the cliff that fell down to the cruel sea below. Dermod was getting weaker and was about to beg for mercy, when all of a sudden his brother's foot caught in the tangled fern, and they fell with poor Carrick rolling over the edge of the cliff. Staring death in its hideous eyes, Carrick clutched at the tough, short bushes on the brink of the cliff edge. For a few awful seconds he looked up at his brother. Calmly his brother walked forward, raised his foot and brought it down hard on Carrick's hand. With a cry of 'Cain!' upon his lips, Carrick lost his grip and fell to the sea.

As the waters closed around him, his whole life came back before his eyes: the memories of his true love, Nelly and their first meeting, and his promise to her to return. The frowning face of Black Dermod came between them; and then the dark waters sank in his ears and mouth and all remembrance faded; with the voice of his beloved Nelly calling to him, consciousness left him.

The end of the month came and Dermod claimed his bride. Nelly had heard nothing of her lover, the officers were ready to take her poor father to prison, and she allowed herself to be led to the little village church by the man she detested and who, unbeknownst to her, had murdered her one true love.

Father Michael paused from his story and asked his companions, 'Was she to blame? Was she false to her love? Ah! How many innocent young girls have been sent as victims and sacrifices up the altar, to save some father or brother from disgrace! Surely the misery of such martyrdom is a sufficient punishment for the heartaches they have caused. Who will try to judge, when a girl has to choose between her lover and her kindred?' The young men agreed with the old priest and there was a sorrow in their hearts as they beckoned Father Michael to continue.

On he went, describing how the chapel was decked out with all the mockery of gaiety, flowery garlands were twined round the pillars, roses were scattered on the path as the bridal party entered that holy place. Among the spectators was Mr Winthrop and several of the gentlemen from the yacht, who quietly took their places without causing surprise, as one of the sailors had informed the villagers of their wish to witness the ceremony. The bride appeared with her father, surrounded by her family; she was pale and trembling. The weight of heavy sorrow seemed to have added years to her young pretty face. Dermod advanced to her, and the priest was about to commence the service, when from among the strangers dressed as a sailor, Carrick stood up and stepped between the bride and groom. He held Nelly's hand and facing his brother said, 'I have come to claim my bride'. With a blasphemous yell of hatred, Dermod rushed from the church as Nelly fell fainting into her lover's arms.

The wedding ceremony continued, only with Carrick as the groom. A boat from the yacht had rescued him as he was sinking for the last time. The shock of it all had brought on a fit of illness that confined him to bed for several days. But Mr Winthrop's personal doctor had taken good care of the young man. There was now a great joy in the air as all the lads and lasses danced merrily that evening in the old barn at O'Hara's farm; and before the yacht left Ireland, Nelly consented to go to America with her new husband.

In the New Country, fortune followed Carrick and he became one of the most opulent in the Far West. Nelly adored her husband and, surrounded by her many children, she lived happily as the day is long and almost ceased to think with any regret of her home in Ireland.

Two days after the wedding took place; the body of Dermod Dhu was washed up on the shore at the foot of the mountain from where his brother had fallen. And ever since on the anniversary of his death, the restless spirit of Dermod Dhu returns to go through the crime that doomed him to destruction.

The old priest stretched himself and, standing up from his hard seat, explained, 'That is why you saw that struggle; it was the ghost of Black Dermod, damned to relive his treacherous act for all eternity in the Mountains of Mourne'.

The evening was drawing near and the sun was sinking behind the distant hills as the three men slowly descended the mountain together. And as the wind whistled above their heads they thought they could hear the howls of Dermod Dhu, forever trapped in a moment of madness amongst the Mountains of Mourne in the County Down.

19

A POETICAL
DESCRIPTION OF DOWN

I came across this little gem whilst researching this book. The poem was written by Mr Joseph S. Adair who was eighty-two at the time living in Glencoe, Ontario, Canada in 1901. It is a great example of folk art, full of exaggeration and romantic ideals.

I have sung of gay Cork and Dublin's famed towers
  Their classical buildings and bridges so grand,
Their parks and their gardens of fauna and flowers,
    The wonderful pleasure of every land.
  Clontarf and Glasnevin have fame in all ages.
The Boyne and old Derry mark deeds of renown,
  But the glory and fame we read in their pages
Must yield to the beauties of sweet County Down.

The Bann and the Lagan and Mourne's proud mountains
  The farm and the mill and white linen trade,
  Its valleys and hills and clear crystal fountains
  The homes the Scotch-Irish re-settled and made.
  What beauties adorn our dear native county,

From Newry, Rostrevor to Donaghadee
Banbridge and Dromore, with all nature's bounty
Our forefathers planted our true liberty.

The Mountains of Mourne, antique strange idylls
Of Maggie's Great Leap and the dread Bloody Bridge
Where thousands were slain for reading their Bibles
And thrown from the parapet over the ridge.
Newcastle – the watering place of the county
With its baths at the mountains of St Donard's Wells;
Here patients resort from all ore the county
To bathe in their waters, and cull handsome shells.

The Newcastle Beach bears popular fame
Here experts in golf hold annual resort
Where the elite compete in this popular game,
To win loud applause and highest report.
The beauties of nature surpass poet's dreams
From Mourne to Dundrum, the scene's like a spell
The mountains and beach contrast in extremes
Adorned with gay villas and a famous hotel.

The parks and the castle of Annesley and Roden
Adorn Castlewellan and Newcastle stran,
Where horses and phaetons are rapidly ridden
To Loch Islandreavy and source of the Bann.
This beautiful river passes Katesbridge and Gilford,
And enters Lough Neagh at bridged Portadown
Its banks with white linen and lawns are well covered,
'Tis the great staple trade of our brisk County Down.

Downpatrick's old abbey in silence is keeping
The dust of St Patrick for ever held dear,

Around whose lone grave the green shamrock is creeping.
The emblem of 'Trinity', whom Christians revere.
Rathfriland, Dromara, the Ards, and Hillsboro
May prosperity ever their industry crown
And peaceful enjoyment devoid of all sorrow
Still bless the kind peasants of loved County Down.

The schools and the churches of this garden of Erin
Have raised eminent Christians all over the world
All noted for piety, learning and daring,
Who keep Liberty's banner unfurled,
The Dufferins, the Thompsons, the Sloans and the Percys
The Taylors, the Hills and the famed Castlereaghs.
Many patriots of note like the noble De Courceys,
Won glory and honour in troublesome days.

Ballynahinch, Saintfield, Killyleagh and neat Comber,
Kilwarlin, Greyabbey and Donaghadee.
And Bangor's rough shores many beauties can number,
Where stands Helen's Tower on the marge of the sea.
On Hollywood's shores the first Scotch Church
Was erected by Patrick Adair as 'The Bush that still Burns',
Whose light over most of the isle has reflected like-
'Bread on the water', void never returns.

Dear Isle of green Erin, the home of my childhood
Wherever I wander, wherever I roam,
In the land of the stranger, by mountain or wildwood
My heart fondly turns to my dear native home.
Sweet home all the graces and virtues to nourish
May you ever retain your honoured renown
Through all future ages to grow and to flourish
The pride of dear Erin, my own County Down.

20

THE HILLTOWN
FAIRY TALES

There were many local folk and fairy tales collected by a man named Francis McPolin from his native Hilltown in County Down during the 1940s. He was struck by the strong hold that these folk and fairy tales had on the imagination of most of the older generation in the locality. He states that he found that at least a third of those over sixty years of age were proud and true believers in 'The Little People', better known as 'The Fairies'. He found that about half of the remainder believed in fairies but were not open about their beliefs. According to these people the fairies they believed in were not the magical and elaborate fairies that we know from the Brothers Grimm storybooks and such art works as Richard Dadd's masterpiece The Fairy Feller's Master-Stroke. *They believed that the fairies to be just 'Wee People', who seldom grew more than three feet tall, but resembled ordinary human beings in every other way. Their clothing was old fashioned and their features were plain, rather more ugly than handsome.*

Most of them lived in underground caves, having secret entrances in the fairy forts, which may still be seen in varying states of ruin and preservation on most of the hillsides in the surrounding countryside.

The general consensus was that the fairy-world was composed of the original fairy people known as the 'Tuatha De Dannan' or 'The People of the Goddess Danu', and the humans who had been carried off or abducted by them and kept in fairyland permanently. These humans are known as 'Changelings'. It was believed that there were certain times of the year which were quite dangerous in regards to these abductions, 1 May being one of them, and, probably the best known, 31 October. These were believed to be times when the ethereal wall between the human world and the fairy world was at its thinnest.

According to McPolin the following series of stories were told to him by an old storyteller or 'Seanchaidhe' he met from Hilltown sometime in the mid-1940s. Unfortunately McPolin never related the name of the storyteller to us, maybe they wished to remain anonymous as not to offend or upset the fairies who don't like their business being broadcasted. These stories illustrate fairy abductions, human intervention, football, Halloween, fairy trees and various ways to prevent unwanted attention from the little people. I do hope you enjoy this wonderful collection of short tales from a time now lost and largely forgotten.

THE ABDUCTED WIFE

There was once a man living on the borders of Kilbroney whose wife was heavily pregnant. She was due to give birth at any time, so her husband went away to Rostrevor to look for a midwife. On his way home again the poor man heard his wife's cry for help. Her voice seemed to be coming from nowhere and he knew straight away that the fairies were making off with her. Now, as it happened, he had a penknife in his pocket. So he took it out and with the aid of the steel blade he managed to cut the spell and took her off them and brought her home, safe and sound. ('I myself have heard it from respected sources that you must always carry steel with you amongst the enchantments if you wish to break a spell.') When he reached his own door he found all the neighbouring women gathered in the house weeping and commiserating, like they were attending a wake. 'We have terrible tidings for you,' one of them said to him. 'Your poor wife has died!'

'That's nonsense,' replied the man, 'Shur, I have her here with me. She is just outside.'

But one of the women led him into the room and pointed to the bed. And there lay a body that looked remarkably like his wife, stretched out, stiff and lifeless. The man immediately ran outside and brought in a shovel. Then he cleared the floor and made all preparations for shovelling the corpse out of the bed and into the fire, like she were a pile of turf. But at the first touch of the shovel's steel head she flew up the chimney with a terrible shriek and dissolved into the air just like a mist in the moonlight, leaving the house clear for his real wife to return.

THE STOLEN CHILD

Babies often taken by the fairies and the substitutes which the fairies left behind in the cradles were called 'changelings'. The following story tells of how a baby was stolen by the fairies but was recovered and brought back to its mother.

A man called Mick Molloy lived in the townland of Leod. He was married, but he had no children of his own. He was a rich man and he had no need to work for a living. For this reason he lay in bed for most of the day and rambled about the countryside at night. There wasn't a dance in half the country that he didn't go to and take part in. And on his excursions he always took the wee roads and the short-cuts across fields and over shucks, not that he had any particular reason for avoiding the main roads, but he just seemed to like to shorten his journey whenever he could and it made it all the more interesting for him. No one knew their way about the place better than the bold Mick Molloy. Indeed, it was said that he knew every lane and footpath from Hilltown to Banbridge to Poyntzpass.

One night he was going to a dance somewhere beyond Maheral. He walked through fields and over ditches, avoiding the well-trodden paths and roads. And just as he was passing along the end of a field close to the back of a cottage not very far from Maheral Chapel, he spied the fairies carrying a baby out through the back window of the small cottage, ready to take the poor wee thing away.

Bold Mick reached up his hand to the window, took the child in his arms and carried it home to his wife. He told her all about where he got the baby from and, as it was a well-known fact that most babies stolen by the fairies were nearly always taken from neglectful homes, between them they decided to rear it themselves.

Well a while later Mick found himself on his way to a dance in the same part of the country and, going along by the same way as before, he came to the back of the very house where he had found the fairies stealing the baby. Out of curiosity, he decided to go inside for a moment and see what sort of place he had saved the child from. As he stepped over the threshold he caught sight of a woman sitting by the fireside, weeping uncontrollably. Beside her chair there was a cradle, and in the cradle an ugly, bold-looking child, roaring and screaming for all the heavens to hear.

'What am I to do with this baby at all?' exclaimed the poor woman through her tears. She explained that it was only a few weeks old, but it had big teeth like a horse, and it was so bad tempered and so wicked that it bit her every time she tried to feed it. Mick then explained to the woman, that the thing in the cradle was not her baby at all. It was, he said, a changeling left there by the fairies on the night they stole her child and carried it out through the back window. He then went on to tell her how he had rescued the baby from the fairies and brought it home to his wife. He assured her that the child was alive and being well looked after in the townland of Leod, near Hilltown.

He said he would bring the child back but only if the woman promised to take good care of it and not let the child out of her sight. When he saw the real tears of remorse and despair come from the woman's eyes he knew that she would be true to her word.

Mick did just as he promised; he took the baby and returned it to its mother a short time afterwards. 'But what must I do with this creature?' asked the woman, pointing to the changeling in the cradle with its big teeth and cruel eyes. Mick told her to put the changeling on a shovel and take it towards the fire. As she did this she was to call upon the fairies to come and get their creature otherwise she would throw it on the fire. This is what she did, and just as she was about to carry out the threat, the changeling flew off the shovel and was away up the chimney with a roar.

Mick then placed the real baby in the cradle, and woman thanked him profusely for the great favour and kindness he had bestowed upon her. She remarked on how well her child looked and how well looked after it was and said that Mick and his wife could come and visit her and the child anytime they liked.

MIDWIFE TO THE LITTLE PEOPLE

Once in a while the fairies would take people who they felt would be of use to them for one reason or another and when they were done with them they would bring them back unharmed and often rewarded. This happened once to a midwife known to the locals as Mrs Flanagan, who lived somewhere between Hilltown and Mayobridge. The fairies had got wind of her exceptional skills as a midwife and one night, while she and her husband were asleep, there came a terrible banging on the door.

Mrs Flanagan woke up, climbed out of bed and dressed herself and then proceeded to open the door, thinking it was just the usual kind of call from expecting people. But when she opened the door, standing in front of her was a strange-looking man all dressed in black, standing beside a big grey horse. He said that he had come to take Mrs Flanagan to attend to his wife. He then pointed to a passenger seat behind his saddle and invited her to mount.

Sensing danger, Mrs Flanagan initially refused to go with him. But as the man was in distress and begged her to go with him, she consulted her husband, and finally it was decided that she should go. So up she got behind the man on the grey horse, and off they galloped at a ferocious speed as if the beast they were on was being carried by the wind.

Over the mountains they flew, bounding from peak to peak, leaping over deep valleys and echoing chasms,

jumping over lakes and seas alike, and on and on until at
last they came to a wide road leading up to a magnificent
castle. When they reached the great palace door, the rider
pulled up, and out came six footmen. They helped Mrs
Flanagan down from her seat and took her up a beautiful
marble staircase, into the room where she was needed.

In the room was a great four-poster bed with a beautiful
young pregnant woman in the full throes of labour. Mrs
Flanagan acted without a second thought and helped deliver
a beautiful baby boy. She handed the child to the mother
and explained to her on how to look after the infant. When
this was done Mrs Flanagan was escorted downstairs and led
into a huge, elaborate dining hall. Crowds of people were
seated at tables covered in beautiful, exotic food and drink.
Servants scurried around serving drink and pampering the
guests whilst others stood by, waiting to be called upon.

Among these guests was a pretty young woman whom
Mrs Flanagan recognised at once as a seamstress who once
lived near her but had passed away. This young woman
was thought to have died of the consumption a few years
ago but here she was alive and safe among the fairies. After
a while the young lady quietly moved over to where Mrs
Flanagan was seated and stood behind her chair. Then when
no one was looking she stooped down and whispered in her
ear, telling her not to eat or drink anything that she was
offered or placed before her, or else she would be put under
a spell and forced to remain there for all eternity.

Mrs Flanagan took the girl's advice and pushed all the
food and drink aside and refused to accept any refreshments
whatsoever. At last the man in black with the grey horse was
brought forward again. A footman assisted Mrs Flanagan to
her seat on the horse, the man called out to the horse and

off they flew. Along the same route they had taken on their way to the castle. Over hills, valleys, lakes and seas they went, till at last they arrived back at her house. Then the rider dismounted and having assisted the lady from the seat, he turned about and galloped off, back to fairyland. After all the adventure and excitement the midwife found herself back to where she started, standing at her own front door. She was none the worse for her journey and the pockets of her cloak were filled with gold coins as payment for her services.

The first thing Mrs Flanagan did when she entered the house was to hide the money in an old wooden box, for the fairies had warned her not to tell any mortal soul about the money or what had happened, as they were very peculiar about their privacy. Accordingly, when her husband asked her about what class of payment did she receive, she told he that she got nothing at all. Mr Flanagan found this very hard to believe indeed. 'Ah! Woman you must have got, food and drink and money as payment.' But his wife stood by her story and said that there was nothing to be shown and she demanded they not speak of it again. Mr Flanagan was still not convinced and suggested to his wife that it was all an auld yarn she had spun. Now one would have thought that this was a good thing as the matter was laid to rest and not spoken of again. But Mrs Flanagan could not stand being called a liar, especially by her own husband. So one day, in a fit of frustration and anger, she told him the whole story and to prove it she showed him where she had hidden the gold. She opened the wooden box to show him the gold, but there was none it there. Instead, there was just a pile of ashes where the gold should have been. The fairies, out of spite, and all because she had given away a secret she had been told to keep, had taken back their gold.

GOBLINS IN GOALS

The fairies, like many of us, enjoy a good game of football but they never encouraged human spectators and certainly no human participants. One day in the mid-1800s a well-known County Down character called Oiny Murphy and a neighbour named Mc Comiskey, both of Mullaghmore, heard the fairies playing football. They could hear all the cheering and shouting coming from a wee valley called Rice's Meadow one lovely, clear, moonlit night. The pair of boys headed down the valley to witness the game but when they reached the pitch they saw nothing. Instead they could hear the very same crowd kicking a football, cheering and shouting away up on Leod Hill. So Oiny Murphy and his friend hit the road for Leod. But when they got there the cheering and shouting had shifted to the Glen of Mullaghmore, behind them. By this time Oiny and his companion came to the conclusion that the fairies intended to keep them moving from place to place all night. So they decided that the best thing to do was just go home.

But on his way home, poor Oiny had the misfortune of wandering into a fairy ring nearby and found himself being lifted up into the air as if by magic. He landed on his behind and saw he was surrounded by the wee folk playing their game of football. A keen footballer himself, he jumped up, took off his coat and began to kick with the rest of them. Oh! The craic was mighty. The fairies were cheering him on as he kicked, passed, tackled and even scored. And the fairies were shouting 'Come on Oiney!', 'Good man Oiney!', 'Fair play to ya Oiney!', 'Great goal Oiney!' and all that sort of thing. Shur Oiney was in his element; he thought he was the King of the Fairies.

When the game was over he put on his coat and headed towards home, the fairies kept pace with him. They hopped and skipped around him all the way until they came to a big ditch or shuck, as it's known as in the County Down. Then they all closed in on him and when they had him on every edge of the shuck they shoved him into it. And there was poor Oiny, up to his neck in dirt and filth, not knowing what happened. He could hear the wee rogues tittering and laughing in the distance but they were nowhere to be seen. When Oiny scrambled up, there standing with his mouth agape was his friend Mc Comiskey. 'What happened you?' he asked, 'You were behind me one moment and the next you're standing up to your neck in dirt in a shuck?' Apparently Oiny had only disappeared for just a couple of seconds but he didn't bother trying to explain and the two walked home together on that moonlit night.

FAIRY FESTIVITIES

The most important festival of the year for the fairies is of course Halloween. It is also the time of the year when the ethereal wall between our world and the fairy world is at its thinnest. It has been celebrated in this country for hundreds of years and in the old days people would create 'Jack O' Lanterns' by hollowing out and carving faces into turnips and then putting a lighted candle in them and placing them in the window frame to be seen by anyone or anything looking into the abode. This was to keep the likes of the fairies at bay and protect the house on 'Oiche Shamhna', which translated means 'Night of the Samhain'.

When the Irish emigrated to America they took all their old customs and beliefs with them and Halloween being a big part of Irish tradition, the Jack O' Lantern was a must. But they had no turnips so the very impressive pumpkin made an admirable substitute. And now all over the world the 'Jack O' Lantern' is as synonymous with Halloween as the Christmas tree is with Christmas.

The 'Trick or Treat' ritual also comes from the fairies of Old-Ireland for every Halloween Night the Irish people would leave out wee gifts of food and drink for the fairy folk. And those who refused to do so had tricks and worse bestowed upon them and their livestock.

PETER AND THE FAIRY HORSEMEN

Sometime during the early 1800s a man called Peter Malone lived on the corner of where the Stang road meets the Castlewellan road in County Down. One Halloween night he was coming home from visiting some friends for the craic. It was a beautiful moonlit night and as he hurried along home he could hear enchanting music coming from a field a short distance from the roadside. He paused for a moment to listen and heard a chorus of voices singing:

> 'Saddle and Bridle; Saddle and Bridle,
> Saddle and Bridle; Saddle and Bridle.'

As he listened he found himself joining in:

> 'Saddle and Bridle; Saddle and Bridle,
> Saddle and Bridle; Saddle and Bridle.'

In an instant he was surrounded by a group of fairies on horseback. One of them led up a grey mare with a saddle on its back and a bridle on its head and ordered Peter to climb up on the horse. So up jumped Peter and off they galloped, the whole company riding alongside them. And they rode like the wind over hill and dale, river and lake, mountain and crag and great oceans. They never slowed down for a moment and soon they arrived in the land of sunny Spain. On and on they galloped over dry barren land, high rocky mountains and through deep valleys until they came to a large town. Pulling back their bridles, Peter and his fairy fellows trotted through the town with great ease until they caught up with a funeral procession heading towards a magnificent church in the centre of the town. Peter and the fairies followed the cortege and eventually climbed from their horses and marched respectfully into the church behind the coffin.

They took their places in the church and looked on as the priest recited the prayers. Then someone called out, 'Who will lift the offerings?' At this the chief mourner pointed to Peter. So he took the plate and collected the offerings. When this was done he sneakily put the money in his pockets. And just as he was slipping the last coin into his pocket he found himself standing in the doorway of his own house back in Stang, with his coat bulging with money. It was well into the night now and all his family were asleep in their beds and all the doors and windows securely fastened.

Peter knocked softly on the door and after a while his wife opened it. When she saw it was him she started to give out to him for being out gallivanting till all hours. But Peter was not fazed by this at all and told his wife to calm down for he had pockets full of gold all the way from Spain. He put his hand in his pockets and grabbed a handful of it to show his wife, but to his dismay he found that all he held was a handful of stones. Peter thought he was being very cute treating himself, only to be tricked by the greatest tricksters of all, the fairies.

To Gladden or Sadden the Fairy Folk

The following is an excerpt from 'The Fairies' by William Allingham (1824-1889):

Up the airy mountain,
Down the rushy glen,
We daren't go a-hunting
For fear of little men;
Wee folk, good folk,
Trooping all together;
Green jacket, red cap,
And white owl's feather!

Down along the rocky shore
Some make their home,
They live on crispy pancakes
Of yellow tide-foam;
Some in the reeds
Of the black mountain lake,
With frogs for their watch-dogs,
All night awake.

By the craggy hill-side,
Through the mosses bare,
They have planted thorn-trees

For pleasure here and there.
Is any man so daring
As dig them up in spite,
He shall find their sharpest thorns
In his bed at night.

There are many stories about how people have managed to both offend and please the fairies. The most common are related to folk wandering obliviously into fairy forts or fairy rings. The most heinous of crimes against the wee folk is to damage, disturb or cut down a fairy tree or fairy thorn, which is more commonly known as a whitethorn. These were believed to be watchtowers to the fairies and they used them to watch over the land to make sure that it was safe for them to go out and dance, play, make merriment and mischief. The roots of the fairy tree lead down to the fairy-world below the earth. These trees are in great abundance all over County Down. They are considered sacred and believed to possess great power. Even today if a farmer has one or more on their land they will do nothing to disturb it. There is a magnificent fairy tree in the townland Ballyward on the road between Banbridge to Castlewellan, that has its very own wall around it to protect it.

JACKASS ATTY

This is a story of a farmer known locally as Atty Jack who had his home not far from a fairy fort in Bushtown, in the townland of Ballynanny. One night he and his brother were sitting in the corner of their house, smoking their pipes, listening the wind whistling outside and enjoying the warmth and comfort of the big turf fire. All of a sudden they heard a pitter-patter on the roof above them.

'What's that?' shouted Atty, who was a short-tempered sort of a fellow.

'Ah shur 'tis the fairies dancing,' replied his brother, quite relaxed. 'Don't be meddlin' with them. Leave them be and they'll do the same.'

But it was not long before the pitter-patter turned into a clitter-clatter and then a bish-bash-bang! Now that was it, Atty had had enough, and before his brother had time to stop him he roared out, 'Will ye get away ower that wi' yez!' That did the trick. The dancing stopped at once and there was not a sound from the roof after that.

'You shouldn't a done that Atty!' cried his brother, dropping his pipe. 'Don't you know it's fierce unlucky to meddle with the fairies.'

'Aw! Only an ass would pay attention to that nonsense!' was Atty's reply.

But that was not to be the end of it at all, for the very next morning, when Atty greeted his brother at breakfast, he was taken aback by the look of horror on his brother's face.

'What's up with you boyo?' exclaimed Atty.

'Oh! I knew it, I knew it,' cried the bother as he pointed out the donkey's tail protruding from the small of Atty's back and the big pair of donkey's ears sticking out of his head. The fairies had made a right ass out of him alright!

KEEPING THE FAIRIES SWEET

None of the old folk around Hilltown would have dared speak ill of the fairies and certainly would not have taken Atty's attitude on it. Whether they liked the fairies or not the old folk took great care not to offend them. Indeed they always made sure to speak well of the fairies, especially if they suspected they might be listening. Great prudence and caution was exercised when speaking of the fairies and they were referred to in conversation as 'the good wee people' or more precisely 'the good neighbours'.

It was very common for the old people to try and keep the fairies sweet by giving them gifts of food and drink. One old lady in Hilltown remembered when she was a wee girl her mother used to leave a bowl of porridge in the bushes every night before she went to bed. And when a cow calved she would pour the first bucket of milk on the ground at the root of a fairy tree near the house to ensure no harm would come to the calf or its mother.

I recently met an elderly woman from County Down (who wished to remain anonymous) and she told me that when she was a young girl and whenever there was a pot of tea made it was always left to brew for a while beside the open turf fire. But before anyone took a cup of tea for themselves the host would pour the first drop outside the back door. It was said that these were for the fairies. It was said that if you did not do this and took the first drop for yourself it tasted of smoke and burnt turf and was not fit for human consumption. You had offended the fairies!

Keeping the Fairies Out

Whenever a fairy hell-bent on creating mischief and trouble entered a home it took great discretion, tact and skill to get him to leave. He would never take a hint; and to simply ask him to leave would only make him more malevolent. If you dared to physically throw him you would be guaranteed bad luck and misfortune.

The only safe procedure was to stare for a moment out the front door in the direction of a fairy fort and cry out 'Oh my, the fort is on fire' or if there was a fairy tree outside, you would say 'Some rogue is trying to cut down the fairy tree!' On hearing this, the fairy would jump to his feet and be out the door like a shot. But as we all know, prevention is better than cure. And there are some very simple ways to keep fairies out of your house. One of the best ways is to keep some water in a pot by the door. As long as there was water in the house no fairy dared cross the threshold without permission.

To this day many folk believe in the fairies and not just people from the countryside. I myself for one would not take a chance with them, my own grandmother was a great storyteller or 'Seanchaide' and I grew up listening to stories about their deeds and doings. I was always told to show them respect and never underestimate them. My grandmother had a wee poem she would say about them:

Cut down the fairy thorn
And you'll wish
You were never born!
Fill up the fairy-well
And you may
Ring the funeral bell!

THE FAIRY TREE

I have lived in and around County Down for many years now and I have always been impressed by its natural beauty and magnificent landscape. But one of the most outstanding and familiar sights in this county is its sheer abundance of fairy trees or fairy thorns, also known as the 'Crann na Sióga' but more commonly called the whitethorn.

As a storyteller I have tried to gather as many tales as possible about these magical trees but I have only ever managed to get wee snippets or the same stories repeated over and over about different trees. So I took it upon myself to come up with a tale about such a tree based on what I have heard and learnt about them. This is a tale that I tell to young and old people all around the country.

By the craggy hill-side,
Through the mosses bare,
They have planted thorn-trees
For pleasure here and there.
If any man so daring

As dig them up in spite,
He shall find their sharpest thorns
In his bed at night.

(From 'The Fairies' by William Allingham)

There was once a farmer in who lived in a remote part of
County Down with the Mourne Mountains overlooking
his land like an army of mighty, vigilant sentries. He
was known to all the people for miles around as 'Farmer
Willy-Spud-Murphy-O'Horrible'. He had a face on him
that could turn a sunny Friday afternoon into a miserable
Monday morning and he was so mean he wouldn't even
spend Christmas. He was a terrible man with a great
disregard for the well-being of others and the world around
him. He had two great loves in his miserable life: his land
and his money. He hated everything else, especially anyone
being on his land, trespassers were a scourge beyond
redemption as far as he was concerned. Now of course it
is only right that one would have issues with trespassing
but in this man's mind any living thing that was not paying
rent or working for him on his land, was considered
a 'trespasser'.

Now every day Willy-Spud-Murphy-O'Horrible would
walk across his many acres of land, inspecting and taking
account of his property. He loved his land, but not with
compassion and understanding like true love should but
with a possessive sense of entitlement. On one occasion
he saw a little nest perched in one of the many oak trees
that grew on his land. Inside the nest a brood of chicks
had just hatched. Their little heads pointed skyward,
beaks open wide, waiting for their mother to come and

feed them. 'Cheep, cheep, cheep!' was all that could be heard coming from them. O'Horrible looked up at them, totally disgusted. 'Cheap!' he roared, 'Nothing is Cheap and certainly not rent, and you're not paying any! Get off my land!' With that, the old farmer picked up a large stone and threw it at the nest. The nest flipped over and the chicks fell out, however, one managed to hold on with its beak and the rest held onto him, dangling from each other's legs, swinging like trapeze artists in the wind. Luckily, the mother heard the commotion and got back just in time to swoop down and gather up her children. O'Horrible laughed mockingly and shook his fist at the little creatures. 'I'll make stew out a yez!' he hollered. The birds all got away, shaken but safe, to build a new nest in a more hospitable environment.

As one can imagine, when the farmer found children playing on his land his behaviour was even worse. He roared and screamed and shouted like a man possessed. He jumped up and down and waved his arms about like a chicken dancing on a hot griddle. And the curses and swears out of him would have made all the angels in Heaven weep tears of despair. If he caught the poor children he would take their shoes, claiming that the grass stuck to the soles belonged to him. At least this gave them an opportunity to run away.

Now on his many excursions about his land, O'Horrible would take great pride in visiting his prize field. It was filled with emerald green grass and it had heather growing in the hedges that filled the air with the most wonderful perfume. But right in the middle of this beautiful field stood a fairy tree. O'Horrible hated it with a passion and, even though it had stood there for generations and he had been warned by his father and grandfather (as they too had been warned by their fathers and grandfathers) never ever to harm or cut down the sacred fairy tree, O'Horrible decided to get rid of it. He looked at the roots and all the way up the trunk and right up to the tips of the branches. 'You're the ugliest thing I have ever seen,' he sneered. 'You grow no fruit and you pay no rent. You'll have to go!'

So off he went back to the farm to get his axe and fetch his poor bow-backed horse 'Sorrow'. Sorrow was once a magnificent race horse called 'Sasta', which means satisfied; he had an injury that forced him to retire from racing. His owner had fallen on hard times too and had to sell the horse. O'Horrible had spotted the horse at the mart and paid the lowest price he could to the animal's poor owner. He took him back to his farm where he broke his spirit and crushed his soul so that eventually the animal would only answer to the name Sorrow as Sasta seemed to burn his ears like a mocking jeer. He was made to sleep on a hard stone floor in the old leaky shed where the wind whistled through it and all he had to eat was rotten cabbage.

O'Horrible whipped the horse as it dragged a rickety old cart back to where the fairy tree stood. 'Halt!' shouted the old farmer. He raised the axe above his head, and then he brought it down with a mighty thud. There was a clap of thunder and a flash of lightning and the sky filled with dark angry clouds. There was a terrible silence as if the whole world had come to a standstill. The birds stopped singing, the wind stopped blowing and the water in the nearby river stopped flowing. It was so quiet you could hear a pin drop. Sorrow the horse looked up with sad eyes at the sky and snorted mournfully, knowing that something terrible had just happened. The farmer, oblivious to the changes all around him, brought his axe down hard again on the trunk

and with that the tree fell hitting the ground with an awful crash.

The farmer chopped up the tree for firewood there and then and loaded it onto the cart. He struck poor Sorrow, forcing him to drag the ill-gotten bounty back to the farmhouse. Sorrow was put back in the drafty, leaky shed with no dinner and the old farmer brought some of the wood inside the house. He lit himself a big fire, took off his old boots and lit his pipe. The fire crackled merrily, giving off a lovely scented smoke that curled up the chimney while the flames threw shadows on the walls like dancing demons, 'Ahh! This is grand indeed,' exhaled O'Horrible. It wasn't long before he drifted off to sleep.

Soon he was happily dreaming of all the terrible things he was going to do, when all of a sudden he was woken with the sound of an almighty crash. He got such a fright that the eyes popped out of his head and rolled across the floor, then they shot up the wall and flew across the ceiling, finally landing in his pockets. He gingerly popped them back in his head, blinked a bit, and looked frantically around himself, trying to figure out where the noise had come from.

'Who's there?' screamed the farmer in mortal fear. But there was nothing or no one to be seen. Then he felt something tapping him gently on the back and he spun around, his heart nearly beating out of him with the fear.

Standing behind him was a hideous troll with a big bulbous nose, pointy ears a mouth full of teeth like broken tombstones in a graveyard. Its eyes were like bright burning green lights.

The farmer was terrified but mustered up all his courage and demanded what the creature was doing in his house. 'You're trespassing!' he cried.

'O'Horrible,' roared the troll, 'You are the most pathetic excuse for a life I have ever seen. Count you yourself lucky that it was not up to me what to do with you, for I would mash you up into gruel and feed you to my wolfhounds, you little snake.'

'What's this all about?' asked O'Horrible.

'You cut down our tree and used it for firewood!' boomed the troll.

Well now that was just too much and O'Horrible forgot his fears and shouted back at the troll 'Your tree? It was my tree, on my land and can do whatever I want with it. Now get out of my house you ugly brute!'

The troll was furious, grabbed the farmer by the scruff of the neck and carried him out the door. He took him into the night where the wind was blowing furiously and the rain was belting down in sheets. The sky was full of thunder and lightning, it was a terrifying night to be out in. He threw O'Horrible over his shoulder and took him, kicking and screaming, to the field where the fairy tree used to stand.

To the farmer's amazement the tree had magically grown back and was in all its original glory and surrounded by every type of creature from fairyland that you could possibly imagine. There were trolls, goblins, elves, ogres, leprechauns and of course fairies, all dancing and singing, holding hands around the fairy tree. When they saw O'Horrible approaching they stopped and rushed towards him screeching. They all joined hands again and began to dance around him. They were all shrieking and singing a song that went like this:

No Mercy, no mercy
Shall be shown to thee.

No kindness, no patience
No clemency.

Only rage and anger,
Bitterness and scorn,
For you cut down
Our fairy thorn!

The farmer was filled with terror; he could not believe that this was happening. It was just a stupid, ugly old tree after all. Then he felt the dancers squeeze in closer around him and he found himself being pushed hard against the tree. He was being squashed into it! He let out a terrible scream and then there was silence.

The following morning the sun was bright in the sky and there was a great feeling about the place. The fairy tree stood proud and strong in the middle of its lovely green field, the birds sang happily in the trees, the wind whistled a sweet song and the river ran freely like glittering diamonds in the sunlight.

There was no sign of Farmer-Willy-Spud-Murphy-O'Horrible and even Sorrow the horse had disappeared. Before long the people from the surrounding areas started to come to the old farmer's land. They knocked down the house and built new houses on the land. They built a wonderful playground for the children and the land was filled with laughter and happiness. I am sure you are wondering what happened to poor old Sorrow. Well the night that the fairies came for O'Horrible, they took the horse from his terrible shed and brought him to fairyland where they fed him and cared for him and now he runs with the magical horses of 'Tir na Nog' and there he will live in peace and tranquility for all eternity.

The fairy tree still stands proudly in its field and for a while, if you looked at it closely, you could see a gnarled face with a mean expression on it. It was the face of Farmer O'Horrible, trapped inside the fairy tree. But apparently he complained and whined so much the poor fairies could get no rest. They ignored him until one day he apologised for all his wrongdoings and swore he would do anything to make amends. The fairies took pity on him and took him out of the tree and gave him the job of taking care of all the fairy trees in County Down. Sometimes you might see him on a dark night, usually around Halloween, tending and watering the fairy trees of County Down, but believe me you won't find a happier or more grateful man in all of the County Down.

If you enjoyed this book, you may also be interested in…

Ulster, Ireland & The Somme

CATHERINE SWITZER

Ulster, Ireland and the Somme tells the story of the relationship between Ulster, Ireland and the Somme area of northern France, which has now endured for nearly a century. The 1916 Battle of the Somme is a key event in the Irish memory of the Great War, and thousands of people from both Northern Ireland and the Irish Republic visit the area each year, but the history of the landscape and the memorials they see has never been told in any detail until now.

978 1 84588 772 8

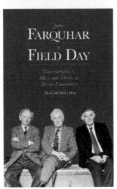

From Farquhar to Field Day

NUALA MCALLISTER HART

Derry–Londonderry has a distinctive cultural history which reflects its unique position in the history of Ireland. This ground-breaking book examines three centuries of music and theatre in the city highlighting the key figures and turning points in its cultural life. It documents the rich diversity of drama and concerts played out in the city's theatres and concert halls, from the birth of playwright George Farquhar in 1677 to performances by the Field Day Theatre Company and the cultural revival of the 1990s and beyond.

978 1 84588 735 3

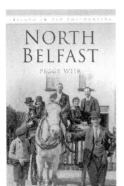

North Belfast In Old Photographs

PEGGY WEIR

This fascinating collection of over 200 photographs reflects these developments and charts the history, character and life of North Belfast over the last hundred years. Chapters showing the churches, schools and harbour are complemented by sections dealing with the everyday life of the people of North Belfast, from leisure and social events to some notable local residents.

978 1 84588 782 7

Visit our websites and discover thousands of other History Press books.

www.thehistorypress.ie
www.thehistorypress.co.uk